D0891151

RIPPLES
A CONSEQUENCES STAND ALONE NOVEL

ALEATHA ROMIG

Edited by LISA AURELLO
Cover Art by KELLIE DENNIS COVER BY DESIGN
Formatting by ROMIG WORKS LLC

ROMIG WORKS LLC

RIPPLES - A CONSEQUENCES STAND-ALONE NOVEL

By New York Times, Wall Street Journal, and USA Today bestselling author Aleatha Romig

COPYRIGHT AND LICENSE INFORMATION

RIPPLES – A Consequences Stand-alone Novel

This is a work of fiction. Names, characters, places, and incidents either are the product of the author's imagination or

~

"Just as ripples spread out when a single pebble is dropped into water, the actions of individuals can have far-reaching effects."
~Dalai Lama

~

RIPPLES
A Consequences Standalone Novel

Wall Street Journal, New York Times and USA Today Bestselling Author

Aleatha Romig

You don't have to read the Consequences series to enjoy this stand-alone novel, but if you know Tony Rawlings, you know that disappointing him isn't an option. Imagine being his youngest daughter...imagine telling him the unimaginable...

"Those who don't know history are doomed to repeat it."

Sometimes ideas find you, and dreams begin as nightmares. Sometimes the truth that has been kept hidden is the key to opening a door you never knew existed.

"You might not know me. I'm the baby of the Rawlings family, the princess, the daughter who came along later. I'm not like my older siblings, successful at everything they touch. My mother and father have provided me with every luxury as well as their unyielding love and support, but I'm not spoiled. I'm also not content. By example, my parents have shown me how love should be. I don't know their past, and that doesn't matter. I know what I've seen—two people devoted to one another.

I don't believe that I'll ever find that kind of love, the kind that forgives and accepts all. And as my life falls to pieces and I travel to visit my family to face their disappointment, I'm not even looking for it.

I'm looking for an escape...from my life as a Rawlings...from the pressure to achieve and not let others down. I dream of the time I can live for my own desires without the expectations that come with my name.

I don't find what I'm seeking...it finds me. Or should I say...*he* finds me.

This time is different. I have a family who will search for me and find the answers. Little do we know—any of us—that my father set my journey into motion long before I was born."

"Just as ripples spread out when a single pebble is dropped into water, the actions of individuals can have far-reaching effects."
~Dalai Lama

Ripples (Unabridged Version) is Natalie's story, the youngest of Tony and Claire's children—their baby. This story first appeared in shorter form in *Glamour: Contemporary Fairytale Retellings*. Due to the length restriction of each novella in that anthology, many scenes in Ripples were shortened or omitted for that anthology. This unabridged edition is the entire story—double in length and—a full-length novel.

Please enjoy this Consequences novel along with special appearances from your favorite Consequences characters.

AUTHOR'S NOTE:

Ripples first appeared in the anthology *Glamour* which contained eight fantastic novellas.

The length of each novella was limited to 25,000 words. As *Ripples* appeared, it was 30,000. Though I had exceeded the word count, there was more story to tell.

This is the unabridged version of *Ripples,* with expanded scenes and additional chapters. The expansion doubled the length of the original novella.

I hope you enjoy *Ripples.* I know I did.

~ Aleatha

DISCLAIMER

This stand-alone novel within the CONSEQUENCES series contains dark adult content. There are situations of kidnapping and dubious consent—there is no non-consent. If you're unable to read this material, please do not purchase. If you are ready, welcome aboard and enjoy the ride!

~Aleatha Romig

A GLANCE INTO THE FUTURE

History is a vast early warning system. ~ Norman Cousins

"Daddy, I want to introduce you to my fiancé."

Natalie's father's brown eyes darkened as he gazed upon the man at his daughter's side. Even at his age, Anthony Rawlings was an intimidating and formidable man in all matters, personal as well as business. Retirement was but a word not fully in his repertoire. He'd built his family's castles and riches from nothing. He'd be involved in their success until he took his last breath.

That didn't mean he was an absentee father. On the contrary, he was omnipresent—as he was in all things.

This greeting, after Natalie's disappearance, was personal and difficult to accept, leaving him and her mother uncharacteristically unnerved. The young woman making the introduction was their beautiful baby, their second daughter, the one for whom the world held fewer expectations. He, however, had plans for her—expectations and dreams—as did her mother, none that included the man at her side.

Natalie's course may not have been as defined as her older siblings, but their stories were for another time. This was Natalie's.

Anthony's shoulders broadened and neck stiffened. Before Natalie could say anything else, her mother placed her petite hand upon her father's sleeve. The diamond ring on her mother's finger glittered with dancing rainbow prisms as her touch gently reminded Tony that this was their cherished princess and apparently, her chosen prince. It was not the time for her father to assert his dominance.

Yet he knew that this wasn't the way it was meant to be.

It wasn't the future they had planned for their baby girl.

Tony's question formed—a demand to know how this union happened. It teetered on the tip of his tongue while at the same time Claire's grasp tightened, pleading for his understanding, if only momentarily. It was truly her gift, the ability to calm the seas without uttering a word.

In the short time that all their gazes locked, the answers to her father's questions and more lurked in the shadows of the present and past. There was more to this man—the one with the audacity to have his hand on Natalie's back—than there appeared. There was a darkness that was all too familiar.

Her father let out a long breath and offered his hand. His

handshake was not to be interpreted as a white flag. Anthony Rawlings didn't surrender.

As their grips tightened, Tony stared knowingly into the eyes of evil. They weren't hard to recognize. He'd seen them often enough in the mirror.

It's a lesson that he knows too well. Some things are better left behind closed doors. Because once the truth is revealed, they'll discover that despite his and his wife's best efforts to keep their baby girl safe, Natalie's consequences were set into motion a long time ago.

CHAPTER 1

BEFORE THE FUTURE AND AFTER THE PAST

When you have expectations, you are setting *yourself up for disappointment.* ~ Ryan Reynolds

The dreary, overcast sky settled around the buildings, obscuring their height as the car slowly made its way through Boston traffic. The holiday break was here. Soon Natalie would be faced with the truth of her reality. All of her father's money couldn't propitiate the cause any longer. Natalie Rawlings's time at Harvard was done.

She'd managed to keep the news from both of her parents, but soon they'd hear it, and as it should, it would come from

ALEATHA ROMIG

her. In today's world, it was a miracle that they hadn't already heard, either from the gossip-hungry leeches on social media or from the registrar's office. Of course, there were rules about confidentiality for adult students, but when it came to Anthony Rawlings, rules were at his discretion.

She'd practiced her speech a hundred ways, yet nothing sounded right. She still didn't know how she would tell them— or especially him—that she'd failed. No matter what she said, her fourth semester as a Harvard student wouldn't happen. She wasn't her father nor even her siblings. The world of business and all that it entailed may be in her genes, but it wasn't in her heart. It never had been.

Maybe she was more like her mother.

Life beyond the walls of expectancy was where Natalie's dreams could be found, a sliver of time where she could be herself—no one's daughter or sister, and perhaps not even a woman she yet knew. There was more out in the world than she'd seen. There were people with the freedom to make their own choices and forge their own trails based upon their desires.

She had desires, ones that she couldn't articulate as if they were an unknown part of her, ones yet to be revealed. The frequency of these thoughts had increased to the point that in her mind they'd moved from ideas to wants to insatiable cravings.

As her classes focused more upon the major her father had chosen for her, her ability to concentrate waned until she couldn't find the ambition. It was lost. Instead of seeking help, she gave in to the inevitable, and now her time at Harvard was done.

Natalie gasped as the car skidded, the wheels swerving on the slushy street. As she reached out and her body lunged

2

forward, the seatbelt tugged her backward. It was a metaphor for her life: any attempt at freedom would be met with a gentle but firm reminder that her bubble served the purpose of safety. She had a designated place. It was where she was to stay.

"I'm sorry, Miss Natalie," the older driver said as his eyes remained steadfast on the road and traffic. "The roads are getting worse."

She didn't respond. The roads weren't her concern. Currently, her flight to Munich and then onto Nice, as well as the conversation awaiting her once she arrived, topped her list.

Beyond the windows, the snow-lined sidewalks provided a simple strip of wet, salt-covered concrete. The pedestrians huddled beneath their hats and coats as Natalie imagined the crunch crackling under their boots. It wasn't difficult. The floorboard beside her feet was white with pellets.

"Miss, Mrs. Rawlings made your reservations. Your first flight leaves in an hour and a half. This traffic isn't helping. I have your passport and boarding passes. You're TSA PreCheck, but you'll still need to hurry. For international travel, they recommend..."

Hurry. What if she didn't? What if she missed her flight?

Her psychology professor may surmise that missing her flight had been Natalie's plan all along. It was the reason she purposely delayed packing and wasn't ready when her car arrived. A less analytical observer would say she was delayed because she'd spent the majority of her time saying goodbye to her friends, classmates, and roommates.

They knew what her family didn't.

Natalie also knew that her mother would be devastated if Nat missed their family time. Nat's choices seemed unfair: go on holiday and disappoint, or not attend and do the same.

Either way, the stress of her failure would be another addition to Nat's growing list of her parents' disappointments.

She thought of her mother. Seemingly fragile yet strong, soft-spoken and yet always heard. Claire Rawlings was as different from Natalie's powerful father as day was from night, and despite that, in her own way, her mother was the true force.

Natalie gave that more thought. If that were the case—that her mother was the force—then why was Natalie on her way to Christmas in France? Her mother detested the cold.

Since leaving the campus, the soft, cool mist beyond the windows had morphed, first becoming pinging ice and then snowflakes the size of quarters. Each transformation further eclipsed the afternoon sun. Even the twinkling lights on the trees lining the streets failed to fill her with the holiday spirit.

If only she could go somewhere else.

Natalie contemplated her packing. She didn't have gifts for her parents. A sweatshirt from the campus bookstore saying *Harvard Parent* no longer seemed appropriate. That was fine; there were plenty of shopping opportunities in Nice.

Nat rubbed her gloved hands as her body shivered. This deep-seated chill wouldn't go away. It was more than her present—it was going to be her future too. A chateau in France, even the South of France, may be a few degrees warmer than Boston but most likely equally as dreary. Usually, as was her mother's preference, family holidays were spent in the tropical sun. What had disrupted the normal plans and why was Natalie on her way to France instead of a tropical location?

If she'd taken the time to talk to either of her parents for more than a few minutes here and there, she might know. Then again, she also might have blurted out the truth of her failing grades. Avoidance seemed the best answer until it was no longer possible.

"Miss? You're very quiet. Is everything all right?"

"No, not really."

"Don't worry about your flight. When you were delayed at the campus, I called the airline. They won't leave without you."

"Of course they won't. My parents?" Natalie asked.

"They're already in France. They flew privately..."

It was how she was supposed to travel. However, being the youngest had advantages. There wasn't much she couldn't convince her father to do or give. She told him she didn't want to fly privately, so she wasn't. The real truth was that she didn't want to fly to France at all.

The driver continued, "I'm sure you know that your brother..."

Yes, her brother, Nate. She'd read something online recently about his amazing feats in the European markets. Years ago, political changes allowed her father a foothold in the EU that according to the article, her brother has recently capitalized upon. Like father, like son.

Truly, Natalie's older sister's accomplishments were no less impressive than their brother's, though her story contained an interesting, if not scandalous footnote. It was something the family never mentioned.

"I'm sorry," Natalie said. "I'm sure I was already told, but will everyone be there?"

"Everyone? Your family will all be there. If that's what you're asking."

More ears to hear her announcement and more eyes to convey her father's disappointment.

The car eased to a stop under the covered entrance before the Boston airport. The driver rushed from his seat and opened her door. Cool air replaced the warmth. She stepped onto the curb.

At least the falling snow was blocked by the roof, even if the cold wind was not. The older gentleman handed Natalie an envelope, *Rawlings* embossed in the corner. "Your boarding pass and passport, Miss Natalie. Hurry through security. I'll check your luggage."

"Thank you, Jamison."

"Miss, I know you expected Mr. Roach. He had some business to attend, but will meet your plane in Nice."

She had expected him. Where was he that he could have been with her in Boston and will still meet her plane in France? The question was fleeting as she realized that Phil Roach would be just another person to look at her with relentless dissatisfaction as she told her story about flunking out of Harvard.

Taking another step, Natalie squinted. Beyond the covered drive, beyond the signs of different airlines, the ground was quickly becoming covered with a blanket of white. "Do you think they'll delay the flight?" she asked.

"No, miss. They know your father is waiting."

Normally he didn't like to wait, but for his baby, Natalie knew he would.

CHAPTER 2

Coincidence is the word we use when *we can't see the levers and pulleys.* ~ Emma Bull

"Y ou made it," the man in seat 2B said as he stood, allowing Natalie to move past him to her seat beside the window.

"Why, yes," Natalie sighed more than said, shoving her carry-on bag into the overhead compartment and making a brief assessment of her travel companion. "Even with PreCheck, the security lines were unreal." Settling into her seat, she looked up. Since the man was still standing, she couldn't see his face. Instead, she started with his long legs and moved upward to his trim waist, firm torso, and broad shoulders. She liked the view, even contemplating that perhaps the flight wouldn't be as bad as she'd expected—until he sat and spoke again.

With his jaw clenched, his words came out harshly. "Why wouldn't you expect that? You should have allowed for the delay. It's the holiday travel time. In a few more minutes, they'll be closing the door. Do you realize that you could have missed the flight?"

His crass tone and cool eyes took her aback. It was as if he were reprimanding her. "Excuse me, do I know you?"

At once, his stern demeanor melted, thawing the ice from his eyes and raising his cheeks as a smile bloomed. He lifted his hand. "We haven't been formally introduced. I'm Dexter, Dexter Smithers."

Years of manners were impossible to forget, even with this man's unusually stern introduction. Slowly, Natalie extended her hand and they shook. His grip was firm and warm, a nice contrast to the temperature outside. "Nice to meet you. I'm Natalie. My friends call me Nat."

"My friends call me Dex," he said, "but to be honest, I hate it."

She laughed. Maybe the flight wouldn't be so bad.

As he buckled his seatbelt, she stole a sideways glance. Now that Dexter's expression had softened, he definitely looked like the type of man she would consider handsome. Probably a few years older than she, with dark blond hair that covered the tips of his ears and blue-green eyes, he had a sexy, suave Norwegian look. When she first arrived, she'd rushed past him so quickly that she couldn't be sure of his height, but based on the fact that he'd tilted his head within the cabin to stand and the way he filled the first-class seat, he was easily over six feet.

Natalie found taller men more attractive. She'd inherited her father's height, towering over her mother and topping off at nearly five feet nine inches. Being a fan of high heels, she thought tall men made the best arm candy.

There was something about him that seemed familiar, as if she'd seen him before. Maybe they'd passed one another in the terminal, or perhaps it was her imagination.

A loud noise drew her attention away from her thoughts to the window. The deicer truck was farther back, shooting something hot against the wing. The snowy air filled with steam as a loud hiss permeated the cabin. "I really hate this. I wish they'd just postpone the flight instead of taking all of these precautions. I don't feel safe."

"Safety is simply a matter of trust. No one is ever really safe. There is always someone else with more power. Besides, postponing wouldn't do. My plans have been in place for too long."

She took a deep breath, momentarily closed her eyes, and leaned back against the soft seat. "I guess I need to trust the airlines. They wouldn't take off if it were dangerous, right?"

"Danger, now that's another concern altogether. It implies harm."

A cold chill scattered over her skin.

"Your plans?" she asked, her eyes now open as she spoke, hoping to shake the strange feeling that this man brought on. She rubbed the arms of her sweater, taming the goose bumps materializing underneath. "Are they for the holiday?"

"The holiday? No, my plans are for much longer than a few weeks."

"Really? Do you live in Europe?"

His lips quirked upward. "Not permanently, but with the

isolation, it seemed like the perfect place to begin. Wouldn't you agree?"

His words left her uneasy. Instead of concentrating on them, Natalie thought back over her various travels. "I've found Europe to be magical—the castles and history."

"Tell me, Natalie." He leaned closer. "I'd like to get to know you better before I call you Nat..."

She swallowed, her mouth suddenly feeling dry.

Where is the attendant?

As Dexter spoke, she scanned the cabin, fighting the restlessness coming to life somewhere below her consciousness. There was something about this man that put her on edge. Something about the intensity of his stare, as if he could call her *Nat*, as if he somehow knew more about her than she did about him. But that was silly. She'd never met him before.

Her imagination was playing tricks. With her concern over facing her parents, flunking out of Harvard, and the cold temperatures in France, she hadn't been sleeping well. This agitation was all part of the stress. If only she could get away from it all instead of flying into the lion's den of her parents' rented vacation home.

"Did you hear me? Are you listening?" His scolding tone pulled her from her thoughts.

"No, I'm sorry. I think my mind was wandering. Have you seen the attendant?"

"I asked you if you believe in magic." When she didn't answer, he continued, "You said that Europe is magical."

"Not literally," she scoffed. "Not as in wizards, witches, spells, and wishes. If those were real, I'd be going somewhere other than France to spend the holiday with my family." She looked around the cabin.

"Where would you be going?"

Her eyes narrowed as her tone took on a hint of sarcasm. "Tell me, kind sir, are you my fairy godmother, or should I say father? Are you here to grant my wishes?"

He lifted his hand and pushed the button near the overhead lights. Within seconds a woman in a blue blouse and skirt with the airline's emblem on her name pin materialized. "Sir, do you need anything?"

"Yes." He turned to Natalie. "What was it that you needed?"

His response surprised her. "Um, a glass of water. Thank you."

The attendant nodded and with a quick pivot hurried toward the hidden area beyond the seats and before the cockpit.

"You didn't need to do that. I was late getting to my seat. That's why she didn't come by. I'm sure she's upset that we're throwing off her schedule." The sound of beeps turned her attention outside the window to where the deicer truck had begun to back away. "We're probably about ready to take off."

Dexter shook his head. "I've never gotten out of Logan flying commercially without at least a twenty-minute taxi. Sometimes it seems as though we're driving instead of flying. Besides, you asked for the attendant. It was your wish."

Within seconds the woman was back with a plastic cup filled with ice water and a napkin. Reaching for the drink, Natalie thanked the attendant and turned to Dexter. "It was my wish and you granted it? So you are my fairy godfather?"

He took the napkin dangling from her fingertips, ran the soft white paper over his palm, before placing it on the armrest between them. "I'm too young to be your father. Go ahead and drink your water. As for the rest of my story, it's a long flight and many hours before we reach our destination." He leaned back.

From Natalie's view, she caught Dexter Smithers's profile—

his protruding brow, high cheekbones, and chiseled jaw as well as the concentration in his stare. The way the muscles in his neck and cheeks flexed as if he were clenching his teeth, as if he were mulling over some serious matter that required his utmost concentration. Despite his lighter complexion and coloring, the look was reassuringly familiar, a focused expression she'd witnessed many times.

After she took a swallow of her water, the plane began to move. She turned his way. Dexter's eyes were open, yet she had the feeling he wasn't seeing what was visible—the back of the seats in front of them, the small screen, and pocket of traveling supplies reserved for overseas flights.

"Is everything all right?" she asked as she placed the cup on the napkin.

He turned her way. With the cabin lights now dimmed, his eyes were darker than before, more aqua blue, the shade that grows darker in the ocean's depths. "I was thinking about what you said. You mentioned history."

"Yes, I've always found European history interesting. American, not so much."

"So things that happened in your own country, even closer to home, don't interest you?"

The plane came to a sudden stop as it joined a line of waiting departures. Dexter reached for the cup of water as its contents sloshed about.

"Thank you for saving my water."

Dexter smiled. "I can't let your wish spill." He pointed toward the window. "It looks as though they're clearing the runways."

He was right. There were numerous trucks with plows, undoubtedly the reason for the backlog of planes.

"I was asking about your interest in things that happened in the past, those things closer to home."

Natalie turned back and shrugged. "I guess that I'm not as interested in that as I am in the royals and dynasties of the past."

"I've found the old adage to be true."

"Which one is that?"

"Those who don't learn from history are doomed to repeat it."

CHAPTER 3

*Neither comprehension nor learning can take place
in an atmosphere of anxiety.* ~ Rose Kennedy

Traveling east as Natalie was doing, away from the sun and into the future, caused the loss of time. Hours disappeared with each mile in the figurative rearview mirror and with each kilometer through the windshield. Different units of measurement couldn't explain the phenomenon. The time in Boston and Munich was never the same. Hours were forever lost, fading into obscurity like the faint cloud of exhaust left in the plane's wake.

Caught within the confines of her first-class cabin, in seat 2A, time accelerated. Nat's body may only have aged six hours, yet the clock ticked faster, progressing twelve hours. As she left Boston behind, reality, too, slipped away.

Natalie watched what happened around her, touched, tasted, and even smelled it. She was never alone. She had help, ever-present, omnipresent assistance. With each tick of that clock, Dexter became more attentive as her comprehension lessened. His hand covered hers reassuringly. He helped her order her meals, even ordering wine.

Natalie wasn't old enough to drink, not legally, in the United States. That didn't mean she never had. She'd had the occasional glass of wine at family dinners and parties. She'd attended parties at school. Yes, even Harvard had those kinds of parties.

Even so, she'd never over-imbibed. She'd seen friends stumble and slur their words. She'd helped some back to their apartment and put them to bed. She'd even assisted with the obligatory ponytail hold. Yet she'd never been the one who lost time, never been the one to wake and ask what she'd done. After all, while her parents were complacent about certain things, other things were unforgivable.

An unforgivable sin was impairing appearance. There were always people watching. A person was never completely alone. That was true of fellow students with phones that could instantly transmit a picture over social networks reaching hundreds, thousands, or more people. That was also true of fake-news organizations that would jump on the story depicting the youngest daughter of a renowned businessman behaving poorly in public. It was even true in her own home. The cameras were for security, but surveillance never stopped.

It always was. Natalie's mother accepted it. Her siblings had done their part to fight it, but it continued. Like the rising and setting of the sun, it was beyond her reach.

Why fight what you cannot change?

That was something her mother told her more than once, something Natalie had taken to heart. It was what it was—learn to accept it. Perhaps it's the reason she accepted her failure at Harvard. Could she have changed it?

As they approached Munich, nearly seven hours after leaving Boston, Natalie couldn't answer that question. It wasn't the only question she was incapable of answering. Simple equations, her favorite color, the name of her first pet...

Essentially everything was slightly beyond her comprehension and thoroughly beyond her articulation. All of the information was just out of reach...as if she were watching instead of participating.

After helping her back to their seats from the bathroom, Dexter reached for her boots from under the seat ahead of them. "Nat, it's time to get ready to disembark."

The boots sitting in her lap were hers; she recognized them. Why were they in her lap?

"I-I..."

He shook his head disapprovingly. "Dear, don't tell me that little bit of wine still has you this confused even after your rest?"

Dear? Rest?

Her eyes narrowed. "I-I don't know you." The words were thick and her tongue sticky. She took a better look. "Do I?"

"Sir, is everything all right?"

It was the woman in blue. Maybe she could help Natalie understand. Yet before Natalie could speak, Dexter spoke. Nat couldn't make out their words though their lips were moving.

The woman smiled and nodded. Nat turned to Dexter; he was doing the same.

The woman leaned down to Natalie. "Congratulations. You're a lucky woman. I'd be celebrating too."

Natalie's head shook, but words didn't form. Not at the necessary rate for conversation. One person spoke and then the other. Long pauses made for uncomfortable silence.

Finally, when Dexter squeezed her hand, Natalie thought to smile—wordless communication. It worked. The woman left.

Wait, was that what she wanted?

"Let me help you," Dexter said, lifting her legs over the center armrest until both of her bootie-covered feet were in his lap. Tenderly, he removed each paper covering, the ones provided by the airlines, and slipped each foot into her black boots. Once they were zipped, he gently placed her feet back upon the floor.

"Thank you," she managed, "...but why?"

"Let me get your bag in case you want to freshen up."

She remembered his blue-green eyes, long legs, and smile. She liked it when the smile reached his eyes. Why did that matter?

Dexter opened her messenger bag, the one she always used for traveling, and rummaged inside. She wanted to stop him, to remind him about privacy, yet the connection was still missing. The words were in her head, but they wouldn't move to her tongue.

Suddenly, a passport was in her hands, opened to the page with her picture.

He leaned close and spoke, his volume low with a tone that bid her attention. "I know you aren't feeling like yourself. That's all right. Look at this." He tapped the information within the small folder. When she looked down, he went on, "We don't have much time. Listen closely and do as I say. Customs should be easy, but they might ask you a question or two. I'll explain that the combination of alcohol and sleep deprivation has you confused, but it's important to know your name."

She blinked, making the words come into focus. "My-my name is Natalie—"

"Your name is Nellie Smithers."

She shook her head again. "No, Natalie—"

"Nellie Smithers." His timbre slowed. "Say it."

"Why?"

He didn't answer, only repeating the name she didn't know, each time slower than the last. She tried to block him out, looking closer at the passport in her hand. It was her picture, but it wasn't her passport picture. This picture couldn't be more than a month or two old. Where did it come from? The picture in *her* passport was taken four years ago, when her childhood passport had expired. In the picture in her hand, she's her current age with long brown hair and big green eyes.

Though their personalities couldn't be more different, Natalie was the spitting image of her older sister, Nichol, if her sister had green eyes. Instead, her sister had inherited their father's brown ones. Nat always thought they made Nichol appear stronger, a more formidable force like their father. That wasn't what her dad said. When he looked at Nat, he'd say that she—his baby—was the perfect combination of light and dark.

Her mom and her dad.

"No...I have a flight to..." She tried to remember where she was going. It was somewhere cold. Her parents were already there. And Nate, her brother. No doubt, Nichol was coming too. "...to...I'm going to..." Her eyelids were heavy, so heavy.

Hadn't she slept? She thought she remembered sleeping.

"Nellie—"

"No, Natalie!" She spoke too loud, too drawn out. People would stare.

Dexter smiled. "That's right, dear. I'll take care of it all."

He'd take care of what? Why was he happy? She'd said Natalie. Quietly, she said the name again, more of a whisper to herself rather than to him. "Nat-lie."

It didn't sound right. She licked her lips. The *T* was soft, though consonants are rarely soft. It wasn't coming out as two syllables.

"Naalie..."

No, that wasn't right.

It was then she noticed her left hand, the rings.

Dexter must have seen her lift her hand because he helped her, raising it higher until the combination of diamonds and gold was right in front of her. "I'm so happy that you like it."

It's a strange sensation when an aircraft begins to slow. Tons of metal, hundreds of people, the weight exceeding anyone's imagination, suddenly decelerating its forward thrust, hanging precariously in the air as if at that moment the aircraft could drop to the earth. It's a frightening sensation—the passengers unable to change the deadly trajectory.

That was the sensation Natalie experienced, a free-fall from a mile high, her stomach in knots. Perspiration dotted her skin, her palms moistened, and the breakfast she couldn't recall eating pushed upward. "I-I'm going...sick..."

Dexter's lips quirked upward; even his eyes lightened. "No, dear, you won't. I made sure of that. The anti-nausea component of your little cocktail won't allow it."

"C-cocktail?"

"Why yes, we're about to land in Munich. You're old enough to drink there. In Germany, it's sixteen for beer and wine. It's eighteen for spirits. The laws are the same at our final destination. Though I must say, as your husband, I'll need to keep a close eye on your intake. It does seem as though you have a rather low tolerance."

There was too much in his speech, so much to decipher.

"Destination?" Her chest clenched. "M-my mom...France."

"Yes, it's interesting that she's who you mention. Of course, one day we'll visit. Keeping us from your family isn't my goal. I doubt our visit will be in France. You won't be ready. Besides, they're only renting that chateau. I'd love to visit their island. I'm sure it's beautiful. But first, don't you think we should get to know one another better?" His hand splayed over her thigh, the heat transcending the material of her tight jeans. "My dear wife."

CHAPTER 4

*Acceptance doesn't mean resignation; it means understanding
that something is what it is and that there's got to be a way
through it.* ~ Michael J. Fox

With each second that Natalie stared, unsure what to
say, Dexter's hold intensified until the tips of his
fingers blanched with the depth of their grip. Pain ached deep
below her skin.

Dropping the passport, she clawed at his unmoving hand.
"Stop. Y-you're hurting me." The sentence came faster, the pain

returning her ability to speak, yet through clenched teeth, the words were barely audible.

Dexter's hand didn't move. The pressure neither lessened nor increased. His words, however, were clear and concise, knives cutting through the plane's rumbling. "On this plane, with the roar of the engines, our conversation is private. Can you remember to keep it that way when we're off the plane?" His fingers dug deeper.

Natalie gasped, biting her lip to keep from screaming. "Please."

"Questions are to be answered the first time."

Her mind swirled as she tried to comprehend his words and somehow ignore the pain. Biting her lip, she nodded.

The pressure increased.

"Please...I can remember."

Again, the pressure leveled. With each assertion, she prayed that he wouldn't make it worse. She could bear it as long as there wasn't more.

"Tell me your name," he demanded.

She tried to remember. Everything was still foggy. The answer was in the passport. Not the real answer, but the one that would bring her relief. The small folder was now wedged beside her leg where she'd dropped it.

Dare she let go of his hand to look?

Before she was able to open it, Dexter snatched the passport with his other hand. The one on her thigh never twitched or wavered in its mission.

"I-I can't remember," she admitted.

Dexter's head slowly shook. His fingers dug harder into the jeans, into her leg.

Tears prickled to life behind her eyes.

"No," he growled, a low rumbling hiss. "That won't do. We

have customs soon and a car to secure."

"But...I have another flight."

"Don't be silly. Europe is too beautiful, and what did you call it? Oh, I remember...magical. It's too magical to miss seeing the countryside."

"I don't understand," Natalie replied, keenly aware that somehow she'd grown tolerant to the pain his hand continued to inflict.

"Your name?"

Her eyes closed to her silent plea. She begged for magic and so much more, the words only audible within her own head. And then she opened her eyes.

Europe wasn't magical, or at least its airspace wasn't. This man—the one she barely knew—was still before her. She'd wished him away. She wished she'd done as her parents wanted and flown privately. She wished she'd never met him, but there he was, his deep-ocean-aqua eyes growing darker and deeper by the moment, staring back. Not staring—demanding. His fingers continued to dig, probing into her skin.

As her breaths hastened, Natalie moved her eyes from side to side, looking...searching. The couple on the other side of the aisle was too interested in one another to notice what was happening. The attendant walked back and forth, seemingly unaware. The people in the seats in front of them spoke, but she couldn't hear what they said. That meant that those near them couldn't hear Dexter either.

No longer prickling, tears teetered on her lids as she asked the questions churning in her stomach, knotting her insides. "Why are you doing this? Are you going to hurt me?"

Dexter's chest expanded and contracted as he leaned even closer.

This man was bigger than she remembered. Wider, stronger. He dominated her vision.

His eyes scanned to where his fingers grasped her thigh and back. "The *why* can wait. Tell me, am I hurting you now?"

If she weren't watching his firm lips, she might not have heard his question phrased and spoken in barely a whisper, but she was watching. Her thoughts were once again forming words and her brain was functioning. Synapses were firing. It wasn't at full speed, but it was there.

Her neck straightened as she answered, "Not as much as at first."

"Explain."

"At first, it might have been shock, but now the intensity...I don't know..." An unwanted tear escaped to her cheek, revealing her lie.

He *was* hurting her.

Still not releasing her thigh, Dexter wiped the tear with a satisfied grin. "The thing is, Nellie, I've slowly increased my hold. Your ability to accept what I'm giving you excites me more than you know."

What the hell? He had? Nellie?

Before she could form a question, he continued, "Will I hurt you? I'm leaving my mark. I plan to leave more. The intensity, your ability to handle what I give, is at your discretion as are your responses and your honesty. Don't lie to me again. Am I hurting you?"

Her head barely bobbed. Admitting was as bad as the pain. "Y-yes."

His aqua eyes sparkled in sick delight at her confession. "Tell me, what's your name?"

She remembered. He'd said it. "Nellie...Nellie..." The twisting in her stomach tightened. If only she could get sick, she'd vomit all over him. But he'd planned for that. What else had he planned?

"Go on."

Her heart beat like a drum, pounding out a distress signal that no one but she heard. "My name is Nellie Smithers." When he didn't respond, she added, "Please."

"Please, what? My dear wife, what are you asking?"

Only her eyes moved, looking down again at the blanched tips of his fingers dug deep into her jeans and skin.

"In the future, we'll work on using words, but for now that will do." His smile widened as his grip loosened.

As it did, Natalie anticipated relief. Instead, pain shot through her thigh, worse than with his grasp. She lunged forward with a whimper, feverishly rubbing the material of her jeans.

"Yes, you see," he calmly explained, "the sensation of blood returning to starved tissues can be more painful than the pressure itself." He paused, pursing his lips in contemplation. "Consider that food for thought. Be careful what you ask. There'll be times when I'll be more than happy to oblige." His head tilted. "And other times when you must trust that I know best."

Who the hell?

Natalie's eyes widened. The world was becoming clearer though it still didn't make sense. This man was threatening her. He spoke as if they were going to stay together. Was he planning on taking her—kidnapping her? "If it's money, my father—"

"Don't be so naïve."

The blood running through her veins chilled as she considered her options. Why hadn't she flown on one of her parents' private planes? She needed a plan. "I can scream. I won't let you do this."

"Do what, my wife?"

Her tenor slowed. "I'm not your wife."

"Au contraire, every form of identification you possess states that you are. Who do you think will be believed, an inebriated woman or her sober husband?"

Natalie frantically pulled the bag from the floor, the one he'd given her earlier from the upper compartment, the one containing the fake passport. Where was her real one? She dug and dug through her things. Her heart raced quicker with each unsuccessful search. No other passport. No boarding pass for her next flight. Even her phone was missing. "Where...?"

And then she remembered her driver's license. It would prove her identity, even containing her Iowa address. A sigh escaped her lips as her fingers brushed the small leather clutch stowed in the bottom of the larger bag. Surely, he hadn't known about that. It was her golden ticket, the one to her freedom and safety.

Dexter didn't speak as she opened the small purse.

Nellie Smithers. Nellie Smithers.

Her ID. Each plastic card. Everything down to the Amex Platinum card her father had given her had that name. The disappointment was staggering.

"H-how?"

"I realize it was premature, and one day I'll change the first name. I rather like the name Nat—my little bug—and soon we'll be better acquainted. In the meantime, this will help our cause."

"No, *I* got on this plane, me, not Nellie Smithers. The airlines will have record. My father will—"

His finger touched her lips. "If you think for even a moment that I haven't thought of that—of everything—you underestimate me." He roughly rubbed his fingers over her bruised thigh, eliciting Nat's small wince. "I look forward to more underes-timating."

At that moment, the attendant appeared with hot cloths. Natalie looked from her to Dexter and back knowing she should say something. Before she could, being ever the gentle-man, Dexter reached for one of the cloths, unfurled the roll of material, allowing the steam to escape, and handed it to Nat with a smile. "I wouldn't want it to burn you."

She took the cloth.

"Miss, I hope you're feeling better," the attendant said.

Natalie looked again from her to Dexter. Silence settled as the beating of her heart increased. A second and another passed.

Finally, Dexter prompted, "Tell her how you're feeling, dear."

Natalie slowly raked her teeth over her lower lip as her gaze moved between the deep-ocean eyes silently warning her to the woman's kind face. Nat took a deep breath and made her deci-sion. It wouldn't help to make her case in the sky. She needed to wait until there was someone who could help. "I'm feeling much better, thank you."

"Don't worry about it, honey," the woman said. "The altitude and alcohol and a newlywed to boot. Your new husband took good care of you. You're in good hands." She winked. "He said you hadn't eaten with all the excitement. It's a combination we often see.

"And as we promised him, your secret is safe with us. We wouldn't want to start your honeymoon holiday off with a scene. Besides, everyone else was so preoccupied in their own world...don't you worry, no one noticed."

Natalie's stomach sank. She wasn't sure if this was good or not. Appearances were taught to her from an early age. However, if she'd been noticed...

"That was very good," Dexter praised once the attendant was gone. The light was once again in his gaze. "I can either reward you for being a good girl, or slip you more of your new favorite cocktail if you plan to misbehave."

Her lips came together. The hairs on the back of her neck prickled with his patronizing tone and condescending words. She wasn't a little girl to be praised or punished. She also didn't like the effects of the drug: the lack of control, the queasy detachment.

"The choice is yours," he continued. "Customs will go much smoother if you're coherent. I'm also prepared to handle it if you're not."

She ran her palm over her tender thigh as the landing announcement spilled from the overhead speakers.

He lifted her hand and brushed his lips over her knuckles before holding it and rubbing her skin. "You're very beautiful, Nat. I've watched and waited. I've had this day planned for a very long time."

"My friends call me that. We're not friends."

The caress of the top of her hand stopped. His thumb pressed upon the fragile bones beneath. Like matchsticks, they could be easily snapped. Before the pressure became too much, he spoke, "You're mine now. And you're right: we're more than friends. Aren't we, my little bug? That's what I'll call you until you earn back your name."

"Stop..." She tried to pull back her hand, but his hold stayed steadfast.

"I have no doubt you'll do it. You'll earn your name as well as mine. I have the utmost faith. You have your father's determination and your mother's submission. It's a fiery combination that I can't wait to explore."

"What do you know about my parents?"

"Everything."

Natalie shook her head as the ring on her left hand caught her attention. It was a large diamond lifted high on white-gold prongs; the band below it was simple. She yearned to take them off and throw them away. In the pit of her stomach, she knew that these rings didn't signify love and commitment, but a collar of ownership.

She hadn't been for sale nor could she be owned. Yet the way Dexter spoke to her was as if he knew otherwise.

"They're not real," Dexter said, releasing her other hand.

"They aren't?"

"No, bug. You'll need to earn that too. And let me tell you, the real ones are spectacular—a family heirloom."

"Stop calling me that. I don't want the real ones."

"You will. And what would you like me to call you?" he asked with a new, unsettling gleam in his eyes.

Her stomach pinched. "My name."

"Go on. Tell me again what that is."

She took a deep breath as another tear escaped and slid down her cheek.

Getting off the plane and avoiding his cocktail were her two immediate goals. Though there was a small part of her that felt a rush from what was happening, the smarter part was telling her to run. Appeasing him would help. She was in control of her answer. Not him. Once they were on solid ground, she'd figure out a plan.

"I'm waiting." His fingertips tapped the armrest, pinkie to forefinger, once, twice. "You should know, I don't like to wait."

"My name is Nellie Smithers."

CHAPTER 5

Things are not always as they seem;
the first appearance deceives many. ~ Phaedrus

As Dexter and Natalie slowly progressed through the customs line, his hand remained in the small of her back, a constant reminder of his presence and expectations. On the surface, they appeared the happy yet weary couple. The reality was more ominous. She concentrated on standing, stepping, and taking in the world around her. The drugs—the so-called cocktail he'd given her—weren't completely out of her system. The effects lingered. Speech was back and, according to him, mobility had never been fully lost. It was how he was able to convince the attendant of her intoxication.

Before they left the plane, Dexter explained the effects of his chosen combination of drugs: lower inhibitions, eliminate awareness, and increase obedience. In a deep, soothing voice, the tone that if others heard would sound comforting, he went on. His words contrasted his timbre, but only Natalie was privy to those.

"But, my bug..."

With the crook of his finger, he gently caressed the line of her jaw, burning her with his touch and branding her with his mark. It took all of her willpower not to pull away.

He continued as the plane taxied to the gate, "It's truly a wonderful concoction. No one in the cabin questioned your sincerity."

"I-I don't remember."

"Of course you don't. That's the problem. If I gave you more for customs, you'd comply with my every command. Honestly, it would make this easier on me." He shrugged. "Maybe even on you. But easy isn't as fun or as thrilling." His hand gripped hers, swallowing it in its girth. "The way you answered the attendant earned you this privilege. Don't disappoint me."

A madman was threatening her and taking her away from her family. He'd already admitted—and demonstrated—that he was willing to hurt her.

She repeated his word as her neck straightened, "Privilege?"

"Why, yes. If I gave you more of your cocktail, you wouldn't remember what's about to happen. How you willingly obeyed, willingly walked to your destiny." The aquamarine irises glittered. "I want you to remember that this was your free will. Don't you want that, too?"

Natalie wanted to forget the entire episode. She wanted to return to Boston, wait for Phil, and fly with him beside her, the man who was

31

more than security, more like an uncle. He would have seen this threat and taken care of it—him—before Natalie even realized it was there. That was what she wanted. Instead, she had to face her new reality and construct a plan of escape.

"Bug." His voice, accompanied by a nudge, brought her back to the large room, the line, and the people.

Reluctantly, she moved, keeping their place in line. With each passing moment, coherency improved. High above, the ceiling was dotted with darkened globes—cameras—recording their movement. Every now and then, she'd look up, hoping that her picture would be recorded. She may have earned this *privilege* as he called it, but this was her chance to end this bizarre abduction before it could go further.

With the necessary forms in the breast pocket of his jacket, Dexter was never more than a few inches away. She hadn't seen what he'd written, only heard his warnings. Even leaving him for the restroom was out of the question. Truly she didn't need to. He'd somehow prompted her to take care of business on the plane, before the cocktail began to lose its grip.

Dexter expected obedience. But she couldn't. If she did as he'd said, there was no hope. The person in the booth was her hope. He or she had to believe Natalie when she said her real name, not the one Dexter wanted her to say.

Nellie Smithers.

The name was in her head and on the tip of her tongue. Dexter had made her repeat it, even write it on a paper napkin as they descended airspace. Surprisingly, the signature she wrote resembled the one on the fake passport and the New York driver's license. He also made her say her birth date. At first, she hadn't noticed the subtle alteration: one month and one year different than her real one. Similar, yet changed.

That was how he'd ordered her wine.

By the time their dinner arrived, the world was fuzzy. Natalie had initially assumed that international flights allowed her to drink at twenty; however, a flight's alcohol limitation was based upon the laws of the country of origin. It was her falsified ID that gave Dexter the ability to ply her with alcohol as well as his *cocktail*.

Step by step, they moved forward. She'd simply nod as he spoke, having difficulty concentrating. She had questions, ones she couldn't ask, but important ones nevertheless.

When was her connecting flight scheduled to leave Munich? Her absence on that flight would set off alarms. After all, she wasn't just *any* passenger. She was Natalie Rawlings and her father was waiting for her arrival. That was what Jamison had told her.

And Phil.

Jamison had said that Phil would be meeting her at the airport. The dread she'd felt at disappointing him with her grades was forgotten. She longed for the security of his presence.

"With your recent change of plans, you would have gone through customs here."

She jumped, startled by the way Dexter spoke close to her ear.

"What?"

He tilted his chin toward the ceiling. "You're making it a point to look at the cameras. Your presence here will neither be considered odd nor unusual."

Nat took a breath and spoke in a low voice. "No. I shouldn't be in customs until France. I don't want my plans to change."

"My bug, that's no longer an option." He nodded toward one of the custom booths. "See that woman, barely more than a girl really, the one who just passed this checkpoint?"

Natalie saw her. She was young, tall, and slender. Her dark hair was pulled back into a ponytail that flowed through the back of a cap. Her clothes were expensive yet average: jeans, boots, a dark green top covered by a light brown sweater. Just before the woman disappeared into the crowd, Natalie noticed her bag: it was one identical to the bag she carried.

And the cap...Natalie wasn't wearing it, but she had one exactly the same.

Suddenly, the room grew warmer, and her skin prickled.

Nat's mouth dried as her knees grew weak. "Why? Why did you point her out?"

"I thought you were smarter than that. You're disappointing me."

There were only a few more passengers ahead of them before they would reach the front of the line. The tears returned as she swallowed the bubbling bile. "She's me?"

"Now there's something you probably didn't expect to say. Who expects to see herself walk away and disappear into a crowd?

"Technically, no, she isn't you. You are you. However, the identity you may be contemplating telling to the man or woman we approach in one of those booths has been cleared to enter Germany. The name you had when you boarded is already officially in Munich. That woman has her—or should I say your—old passport, your boarding pass, all your information." Dexter pressed the small of her back, forcing her to take a few more steps, moving with the line. "The government officials won't believe you if you claim to be her."

Nat's heart thundered as the room teetered. What would happen if she fainted? "I'm the real Natalie Rawlings. My parents—"

"What will happen if you make insane claims? Do you know

the kind of mental facilities they have in Germany?" Dexter asked. "Not exactly as luxurious as the resort where your mother stayed."

She looked up to his face, her mouth agape, as her already-twisted stomach formed another knot. "How do you...?"

Her mother's episode had been ages ago, after Nichol was born and before Nate. It was part of the family history no one mentioned. *The time before* was how it was referenced and by all accounts, there was no need to bring any of it up. Throughout all of Nat's life, her mother was steady and stable, kind and loving. The story Nat had been told was that a traumatic event, combined with an injury she'd suffered in an earlier accident, had sent her mother into what the professionals called *a break with reality.*

What would happen to her mother if Nat disappeared? Could it send her back? Would that be another traumatic event?

Dexter continued to whisper, "I can't help you if they take you away."

Help me?

Studying his expression, Nat assessed her captor. Could she simply outrun him? He was tall, taller than she, possibly as tall as her father, and he was a large man—not fat by any means but solid and hard. Those same adjectives could be used to describe his expression. Solid and hard, as if he were discussing the weather, not her mother's mental health or her own. "But if I disappear, my mom..."

"You won't," he said reassuringly, tenderly rubbing her lower back, his large hand beneath her sweater, yet above her top. To the casual observer, it was a kind, encouraging gesture. "Don't worry, bug. Behave as we've discussed and the other *you* will send your parents a planned text message. You won't disappear.

You simply decided that Munich was as far as you would travel and changed your plans."

"Why would I do that?"

They were nearly at the front of the line.

"Which do you think would be easier for your mother? Her baby girl missing the Christmas holiday because she's embarrassed about her failing grades or her baby girl in a foreign psychiatric hospital after a mental breakdown brought on by the same thing? I mean, that episode on the plane...and now confusion? A case could be made for a break with reality."

She might be having a break. How could this really be happening?

And how did Dexter know about her grades? She hadn't even told her parents. Neither her sister nor her brother knew. "I-I..."

"Come, dear," Dexter said, tugging her hand, "it's our turn. Nellie Smithers," he reminded softly as they approached the booth.

CHAPTER 6

Our lives are defined by opportunities,
even the ones we miss. ~ F. Scott Fitzgerald

"Reason for your visit?" the man with a heavy German accent asked as he scanned the passport barcodes over a light and looked from the small documents to their faces.

Dexter answered, offering their forms and then quickly encasing Natalie's hand in his own. He confidently explained, with just the right amount of detail to sound convincing, that he and his new wife were on holiday—a delayed honeymoon, something about her passport coming with her new name, about castles, snow, and magic. With each word, the gravity of the situation settled around them with the doom of a suffocating cloud—the opposite of his answers—invisible to everyone but her, imprisoning her body and soul as it dazed her vision and stole her rebuttal.

His words sounded innocent and benign. No one but Natalie heard the reality. His speech was a malignant cancer gnawing at her insides and consuming her future.

Though she tried to listen, her thoughts centered on his threat, the one where he said she'd be thought insane. Her mind recalled stories of foreign mental institutions, conjuring images of bleak, lonely rooms with a single cot and no window. She didn't want to believe him.

Mental health didn't hold the stigma it had when her mother was diagnosed. During the last quarter-century, science and medicine had made significant progress, especially in the field of traumatic brain injuries. That was the contributing factor to her mother's episode. It wouldn't be a factor for Nat. She hadn't had an accident. Instead, if she were misdiagnosed, they'd only assume her to be crazy—a family trait.

She wasn't crazy. Neither was her mother. This was all ridiculous. Germany was a modern industrialized country with top-notch doctors who aided in cutting-edge research. This wasn't a third-world country. There were US military installations. The US embassy...

She was a US citizen. A kernel of hope sprouted to life. The officials *would* help her. She just needed to make her case.

It wasn't until Dexter nudged her shoulder that she remembered she was part of the farce occurring around her, assigned with the task of perpetuating his story.

"Time difference and a few glasses of wine," Dexter said to the man, with a laugh.

His chuckle rang with mocked joviality through the air, yet his eyes spoke louder, demanding her obedience and her speech. Her heart accelerated—what was normally one beat became two, if not three. The increased blood flow lacked the required oxygen, making her lightheaded. Maybe if she'd taken the cocktail, this wouldn't hurt as much.

"Mrs. Smithers," the agent asked, "what is your occupation?"

"M-my occupation?" That wasn't a question she'd anticipated.

"Yes, ma'am."

Dexter hadn't prepared her for this query. "I'm a student...I was."

Dexter wrapped his arm around her shoulders. "I suppose that now makes her a wife."

The agent nodded, looking from one to the other. Finally, he asked, "Do either of you have anything to declare?"

Nat began to open her lips to declare her real name. But the agent hadn't asked her name. Why?

He already knew it—the wrong one. He'd addressed her with it, and she'd answered.

Before her words formed, the agent stamped each passport and pushed the folders across the counter. When Dexter reached for their documentation, the agent nodded. "Enjoy your stay." He turned toward the crowd. "*Nächster.*"

"Next," Dexter whispered in her ear, translating the gentleman's one-word sentence.

Next.

Next.

The word rang in Nat's ears as Dexter escorted her into the crowd. A puppeteer was what he was—able to control her simply with pressure upon her back—pulling strings and moving levers. Passing through a large archway, they entered another cavernous room that reminded her of the train or bus stations in big US cities: Grand Central Station in New York, or perhaps Union Station in Chicago. Sounds echoed off the domed ceiling and tiled floor. Though attached to a modern airport, it felt as though they'd stepped into the country's past, into history.

Silently, he led her to a bench where she sat, dejectedly doing as the puppet master commanded. The crowd and commotion faded into a mist of despondency. Voices and faces disappeared. Her hand went to her chest as her breathing labored. Could the mist be poisonous? Or was this debilitating pain physical? Wasn't she too young for a heart attack?

Why wouldn't her lungs fill?

The answer stared her in the face with eyes as cold as the ocean's depths.

His plan was in motion. Stepping away from the booth was her final mistake, her opportunity to stop this—whatever it was —from happening. Her eyes went to the direction from which they'd come as her mind tried desperately to comprehend her dire situation.

Natalie blinked once and then again. Air slowly filled her lungs. Like a fading computer screen, the fog dissipated as the world came back into focus. There were people and noise. She turned toward her captor as he put his phone into the inside pocket of his jacket. If he'd spoken, she hadn't heard.

"Did you call her...me?" Natalie asked.

He kissed the top of her head. "Nothing for you to worry about."

"But my parents, will she text them?"

Natalie hadn't been thrilled about the chateau, but now that it was gone, she wanted it. She couldn't stop the tears as she imagined the scene: waking Christmas morning, the chateau beautifully festive—for her mother loved decorations, her father's deep laugh and mother's approving gaze as they all sipped coffee around the tree. Other people may be there, but through it all, Nat could count on her immediate family. From the moment she arrived, her siblings, Nichol and Nate, would tease her about being the baby. She wasn't just her parents' baby, but theirs too. And now...

Tears blurred the noisy crowd.

Dexter stood and reached for her hand. The scene she'd created was gone. She was back in the hands of this...man.

"No tears, bug. Not yet. Save those for me."

Icy chills scurried up her spine like the tiny feet of a million mice. *Save her tears for him? What the hell?* And then there was the nickname he called her. She wasn't a bug. The moniker grated on her nerves, yet she needed to pick her battles, another of her mother's sayings.

Outside, the wind whipped around them, blowing her hair and chilling her skin. A car was waiting. As they approached, Dexter spoke to a uniformed man in German—another thundering blow. Natalie couldn't ask for help if she wanted to. While she was fluent in both French and English and knew enough Spanish to get by, speaking German was outside her capability.

Dexter opened the passenger side door and gallantly gestured for her to enter.

With her hand on the top of the door, her steps stuttered. She took one last look at the crowd, the bustling world around her, as the cool breeze prickled her moist eyes. Where was she going?

"Your coach awaits you for our magical adventure."

There weren't words capable of expressing her thoughts. Instead, with a deep sigh, she got into the car, settling into the cold seat. After Dexter positioned himself behind the wheel, he offered her a water bottle. She'd watched him buy it, watched his every move. She didn't trust him, not one bit. If she weren't so thirsty, she wouldn't consider drinking what he offered, but she was.

Hesitantly, she opened the cap and sipped, barely enough to wet her parched lips.

With a huff, Dexter took the bottle from her hand, placed it to his lips, and took a long draw. His Adam's apple bobbed as nearly a quarter of the liquid disappeared. Handing it back, he asked, "There, does that make you feel better?"

It did...until it didn't.

He'd taken a drink from it with his lips—his mouth. The small sip she'd consumed percolated within her stomach. It was silly. She wasn't the baby her family made her out to be. She was twenty years old, despite the falsified date on her bogus identifications. She knew what was coming. Drinking from the same bottle would be the least of her concerns or of their connection. Yet if she could fight, she would.

As if reading her mind, Dexter retrieved the water bottle and offered her another. "Here, this one is without my germs. Remember, bug, we'll soon be sharing more than a bottle of water; there won't be a place my lips won't touch."

"My luggage?" she asked, after taking a drink from the new bottle, trying to think of anything but his unappreciated and completely unnecessary verbal confirmation.

"Your layover was long enough. The *other you* will retrieve it. The real you doesn't need it."

She did need it. She may not have packed presents for her family, but her things were there—personal items. Her favorite robe, the one she planned to wear on Christmas morning. Her warm socks and cosmetics. A vision of the packed suitcases showed fleetingly behind her closed lids. How could he determine what she needed and didn't need?

Natalie pulled her sweater tighter around her shoulders and tugged the cuffs over her fingers. Beyond the windows the sky was gray and over the ground was a dusting of snow. "I need my coat. It's in my suitcase." If only she had carried it onboard. Another mistake to add to her never-ending list.

Dexter hit a few buttons on the dashboard, bringing the heat to life, and then shimmied out of his sports jacket. "Here you go."

Tentatively, she reached for the wool sports jacket. Instead of putting it on, she laid it over herself like a blanket. All at once, his scent—fresh and masculine with the addition of his spicy cologne—filled her senses, mixing with the dread of the future. It was a new concoction bubbling in her gut and challenging her sanity.

"Where are we going?" she asked, needing her bearings if she were to plan her escape. As she waited for his answer, warmth flowed from the car's vents. It didn't only fill the air but surrounded her. Had he turned the heater on in her seat? Her eyelids grew heavy. And then she remembered his phone was in his jacket. Maybe she could somehow use it...

The thought slipped away.

He hadn't answered her earlier question. She tried again. "Where...?"

With her inability to complete the question, the realization hit: the cocktail must have been in the second water bottle. She wanted to call him out, but she couldn't. Thoughts disappeared, no longer making it to her lips as she submitted to the warmth and his scent. The world went dark.

CHAPTER 7

The premonitions we so quickly dismiss are sometimes
our truest glances at reality. ~ Richard Paul Evans, *The Letter*

Claire's eyes snapped open. A dream or a nightmare? She peered around their large suite. She wasn't in Iowa. Her heart rate accelerated as she fought the battle between real and imagined. Something wasn't right. She couldn't put her finger on it. It wasn't her location, though this wasn't their home in Iowa. As her eyes adjusted to the dim light of breaking dawn peering around the drapes' edge, she recognized the chateau.

Catching her breath and reassuring herself it was only a

dream, Claire reached for Tony across the large bed, seeking the safety of his embrace. His side of the bed was empty, the soft sheets no longer warm from where he'd slept. The clock on the bedside stand read a little before six in the morning. That was seven hours ahead of Iowa. Traveling always did this to her, messed up her sleep.

That didn't matter. Claire would adjust, just as she always did. What mattered was being together as a family. With Nate's business recently focused in the EU, France was a better gathering place than their island, though Claire did love her island.

There would always be something special about their place hidden in the South Pacific and the significant role it had played in her and Tony's reconciliation. That seemed so long ago. It was—decades now. The memories held just a bit of melancholy. The proprietors who she'd first met long ago were no longer with them. Francis and Madeline had lived their lives out on the small island, tending to the home and caring for the Rawlings, even welcoming each new addition. The new caretakers are equally as devoted, but Claire liked familiarity.

Sitting up, she scanned the large room, taking in the sitting area, the sofa draped with Claire's dress from the night before. She'd been too exhausted to hang it up. If the drapes were open, she expected a gorgeous view of the Ligurian Sea. Slowly, she moved her feet to the soft carpet and made her way to the window.

The soft hues of the breaking dawn calmed her pulse and eased her mind.

As she took in the view of the sparkling sea from high above, she contemplated her awakening—her racing pulse and thundering heart. It was not that unusual. Whenever her family was about to congregate, she worried. Not about the reunion per se, but just the type of maternal worries that infiltrate her thoughts. Tony would tell her that it was silly. Everything always worked out. Yet the mothering side of Claire couldn't quell the concern. Perhaps it was something embedded in a mother's DNA?

She wasn't concerned about their son. Nate had arrived at the chateau yesterday. No doubt he and his father were deep in conversation, even at this early hour, over concerns she truly didn't care about. Having her son home, drinking coffee and solving the world's problems, was what mattered to her.

Nichol was due to arrive today and so was Natalie.

Claire's stomach twisted.

Why had Natalie insisted on flying commercially and more importantly, why had Tony agreed?

Claire shook her head with a grin. Natalie was so like her mother, so Claire. No children wanted to hear that they were the spitting image of a parent, but Natalie was. She wasn't as demonstrative as her siblings. Natalie got her way in everything with her father—in his eyes she could do no wrong—by simply smiling and asking sweetly.

There had been more times than Claire could count that Nichol and Nate's personalities had caused clashes within the Rawlings household. That began when they were young. They each had their father's determination and if Claire were being completely honest, his stubbornness. The waters calmed with time and acceptance.

Anthony Rawlings may never have planned to be a father, but of what Claire was certain was that he wasn't prepared to father himself. That was what raising Nichol and Nate had been like, or as much as Claire could imagine.

Natalie was their surprise, their child who came after they were done having children. With their age difference, Tony was nearly twenty years Claire's senior. He was certain his days as a father to a newborn were behind him. Besides, he was concerned about Claire enduring childbirth again. Though Nate's was an easy birth, both Tony and Claire recalled the difficulty of Nichol's. No one expected a third child. At first, Claire thought she was ill with the flu—she was so tired. The news that she was carrying a third child was amazing and frightening.

Like her brother before her, Natalie Elizabeth Rawlings came into the world without any difficulties. Her dark hair was her father's but her emerald green eyes were her mother's. In those eyes, Claire saw her own reflection and her reprieve. From the first time their gazes met, Claire knew that Natalie was different. She was a Rawlings, but so much more a Nichols. With time, it became more evident. Even at a young age, she was accommodating and a people pleaser, understanding that an expression or tone could change the undercurrent of a conversation. Even with her siblings—who to this day referred to her as the baby—she got her way.

Claire looked again at the clock. Half past six.

Slipping into her robe and slippers, she pulled herself from the glorious lightening view and made her way down to the first level of the chateau.

As she rounded the large column near the bottom of the stairs, the masculine voices she loved came into range. With each step closer, her worries evaporated into the air filled with the scent of coffee, backdrop of surf, and talk of things Claire didn't care to understand.

"...make a move now. The US markets won't open for hours..." Nate was saying.

Claire couldn't stop the smile as she entered the room. Though their conversations bored her to tears, they were always the same. Of course, Nate's father knew the time of the markets, probably better than the arrival time of their daughters.

Stepping closer, Claire went behind Tony and kissed his prickly cheek. His dark hair had succumbed to time, now more white than black. That didn't in any way lessen his handsome appearance, not in Claire's eyes or the eyes of the world. He was often still mentioned when citing wealthy, handsome entrepreneurs. It's a phenomenon with men. They never age, only becoming more distinguished.

"Good morning, Claire," Tony's deep voice took on the timbre it always did when the two of them conversed, reverberating to her heart like a calming wave.

"Good morning."

She ran her hand over Nate's shoulder as she wished him a good day, also. Their son was more and more like his father—in appearance. Though Nate was younger than Tony had been when Claire had first met him long ago in Atlanta, she saw the resemblance and wondered when their son would find that right lady for his life. Truly she wasn't a fan of the women who threw themselves at her son's feet. Had it been that way for Tony in his youth? Claire didn't know. Her life began when they found one another. In her mind, his did too.

Though Nate shared his father's flair for business and all things numerical, his heart was more like his mother's, tender and caring. The combination wasn't a flaw, as he'd shown already in his short time as a world-renowned businessman.

She gave his neck a quick hug. "Have I told you how nice it is to have you here?"

"About fifty times, but I haven't been here that long," Nate replied with a grin. "I'm expecting fifty more before the girls arrive and take up all your time."

"Nonsense. I always have time for you. Where's Phil?" she asked, looking around the large dining table.

Tony's head tilted to the side. "Really? Your two favorite Rawlings men are here, you promise them your time, and you're looking for Roach?"

Claire laughed. "After I pour myself some coffee I am, unless one of you two *favorite Rawlings men* can help me."

"What do you need?" Nate asked.

"To confirm the details of Nichol's and Natalie's arrivals and the plans to pick them up from the airport."

Nate shook his head. "Phil's your man."

Claire winked at Tony. "That's what I've always said."

Tony's dark eyes sparkled. "Taylor's in the kitchen. Maybe you should discuss it with her."

"The girls' arrival?"

"No," Tony said. "Your plans for Roach."

Shaking her head, Claire went to the buffet and poured herself a cup of rich, dark coffee. After adding just the right amount of cream, she left Tony and Nate to continue their conversation that no doubt included world domination—probably before noon.

"What about John and Emily and the kids?" Tony asked before she made it too far.

Spinning on her heels, she replied, "First, Michael is married with a child on the way. I don't think he qualifies as a kid anymore. Didn't I tell you?"

"That Michael is married?" Tony asked. "I believe I was at the wedding. I may be aging, but I'm not senile."

"No." Claire scoffed. "The doctor didn't want Ann to travel. With her due date a little over a month away, they thought it was better to stay in the States."

Tony's smile broadened. "Merry Christmas to me."

Nate shook his head. "Dad! You like Uncle John."

Tony nodded. "Yes, I do."

Claire's grin grew. "He likes your Aunt Emily too, don't you, dear?"

"Yes, dear. Of course."

"See," Nate said, "This is why I'll never marry."

"Just make sure you get along with her family first."

"Tony!" Claire said as she made her way toward Taylor.

The marble floors glistened under her slippers as she followed the hallway. Instead of going directly to the kitchen, she entered the large hall. The Christmas tree she'd ordered was nearly twelve feet tall. As the coffee in her cup warmed her hands, the beauty of the scene all around her helped to continue the settling of her nerves.

The decorations were perfect, not only the tree but also the garland sparkling over the mantel and archways. The large windowed doors that opened onto a stone balcony gave a beautiful view of the glittering sea. One door was slightly ajar, the reason for the sound of the surf below. She continued to splay her fingers over the large cup. It wasn't as warm in Nice as it would be in the South Pacific, but it was Christmas and soon their girls would be present and all would be right with the world.

The door to the kitchen swung inward as Claire pushed the heavy barrier. For an older chateau, the kitchen was amazingly modern with granite countertops and appliances that hid behind ornate carpentry. The cook was preparing breakfast as Claire found the person she was seeking. Sitting at the high bar separating the cooking from the sitting area was Phil's wife and partner in all things, Taylor.

"Claire?" she said, looking up from the tablet before her.

They'd all been together too long for formalities. Besides,

Claire wasn't much for titles. She was simply Claire Rawlings. Her husband was another story. While Phil had been with the Rawlingses longer, once Taylor was added to the mix, their family seemed complete.

"Good morning."

"Good morning. You didn't need to come find me. We can go out to the living room."

"Nonsense." Claire sat her coffee on the counter bar and eased up onto a stool.

"Mrs. Rawlings, may I get you anything?" the woman cooking asked.

"No, I'm just looking for Taylor." She peered toward the large cooking surface. "Something smells wonderful."

"I hope so, madame."

Claire turned to Taylor. "Do you know the plans for the girls? Or should I find Phil?"

Taylor shook her head as she looked back at her tablet. "I've got it. I know Phil promised Nat he'd pick her up."

Claire simply smiled. Nat would get her way no matter who she had wrapped around her finger.

"Nichol is arriving at Aéroport Nice Côte d'Azur at 10:20 this morning. I'll be happy to pick her up." Taylor continued her search of her information. "It appears as though she left the US on schedule. Hopefully she got some sleep during the flight."

Claire watched Taylor, waiting for more. "And Nat?"

Taylor smiled. "Well, with commercial it's not as black and white, but she left Boston yesterday on schedule. Jamison did mention to Phil that she wasn't ready to leave Harvard and seemed distracted."

"Wasn't ready? Why not?"

"I didn't hear any more. I'm sure she'll fill you in as soon as she arrives."

"Did you or Phil tell Mr. Rawlings?" Tony never had an issue with titles or being addressed by them. With him, Mr. Rawlings was about as informal as it got unless you were family or friend, one not on the payroll.

"No. Phil said that Jamison didn't make it sound too urgent. However, it was a close call for her to get to the gate in time, but she did."

"I suppose punctuality isn't one of her strong suits," Claire said, the uneasy feeling from her awakening finding new life.

Taylor continued to read the screen. "...and according to the airline, her flight has recently landed in Munich. Her layover is for two and a half hours. Then once she gets to Nice, she'll go through customs. She should be at the airport about the same time as Nichol. We'll both go, or Phil will pick them both up since he promised Natalie."

"That's great. So she's on the ground in Germany now?"

"Yes."

"Thank you, Taylor. I'll give her a call," Claire said excitedly as she stood, her anticipation growing at hearing her youngest daughter's voice. It was a good thing Claire hadn't told her husband about her worries. He'd have said that she was being overprotective. As if he could talk. It didn't matter. Her heart grew lighter knowing that soon they would all be together.

"Tell her that Phil will be waiting."

"I will," Claire called over her shoulder as she hurried out of the kitchen and back up to their suite to find her phone.

Her coffee forgotten on the counter near Taylor, Claire thought about all the things she and Nat could do together. While Nichol and Nate impressed their father with their knowledge and achievements, Claire and Natalie would enjoy Nice. There were cafes and shops. Even with a chill, they could sit outside and people watch. Just as they had when Nat was a little girl, they would make up stories of the other people, complete with past and future. Those stories were a glimpse into the creative imagination of her daughter.

Claire was certain that inclination led to Natalie's difficulties at Harvard. She undoubtedly took the business track to follow in her father and siblings' shoes. Their youngest daughter had never been the kind for crunching numbers or striving for success. Corporate takeovers may be in her blood, but not in her heart. They would all talk about it after Natalie arrived.

They'd waited for her to tell them, and when it never happened, Claire and Tony decided to give Natalie time before they confronted her.

As Claire reached for her phone, it came to life with the ping of a text message.

Excitedly, she swiped the screen.

"MOM AND DAD, I DON'T KNOW HOW TO SAY THIS..."

Claire clutched her chest as her eyes filled with tears. As seconds lingered in the cool French air, her knees grew weak and she collapsed against the bed as she read and reread the entire text message. Instinctively she hit the call-back button.

The ringing stopped, but no one was there.

"Natalie!" Claire called into her phone.

Nothing.

The line went dead.

Claire's heart ached as she called out to the one man who'd always known what to do. "Tony!"

His phone too had pinged, still attached to the charger at his bedside stand. That was a sure sign he was excited to have Nate here. Normally he'd never be that far away from his phone.

The dread that had awakened Claire this morning with a

start was back, twisting her stomach and accelerating the coursing of her blood.

Though slightly faint, she moved forward and unplugged Tony's phone. On the screen, she saw the same message from Nat's number.

With both phones in hand, she ran toward the stairs. "Tony! Oh God. Our baby. Something is wrong. Tony!"

Dark eyes, the color of molten chocolate, met her halfway to the first floor. He must have heard her initial scream. "What is it?"

CHAPTER 8

*The irrationality of a thing is no argument against its existence,
rather a condition of it. ~ Nietzsche*

Natalie awakened with a start. She was in the moment
where dreams collide with reality at the intersection of
consciousness and unconsciousness, where memories linger
only to be blown away, the end of one and beginning of the
other, the flash where connections blur and lines fade away.

Cold and damp.

So cold.

She huddled closer, tighter within herself, her knees at her chest as she hugged her arms nearer. Heat was the element she craved, yet her body was without it.

Every muscle ached as if she'd been maintaining this position for too long. It wasn't only her arms and legs that hurt; her stomach also cried out. Its need wasn't for warmth but for food. Audible grumblings of hunger echoed off the empty walls.

Where was she and why was she cold and hungry?

Blindly she reached for a blanket, a sheet, anything. Her cool fingertips met a scratchy surface.

Crash! The sound of reality and dreams smashing together.

Natalie's eyes squeezed tighter, and she buried her face into her knees, trying to escape the memories materializing behind her closed lids. If she didn't look—didn't see—perhaps nothing would be real. Yet in her heart and soul, she knew that she hadn't dreamt it or even had a nightmare. The deep ache in her bruised thigh confirmed the reality—flashes of recollections on the plane, in the car, and in a room—that she'd lived it.

Her eyes sprang open as she quickly scooted to a sitting position. Her knees still pressed against her breasts, and her arms now hugged her legs. As she moved, the rough bedding scratched the soft skin of her behind. Despite the uncomfortable surface, she continued until her back collided with something hard. Behind her, at the side of the bed where she'd slept, was a cold painted concrete wall. Like the mattress where she'd lain, its coarse texture abraded her skin.

Her *skin.*

Natalie ran her palm over her bare legs, one and then the other. Goose bumps peppered her body, not only her legs but her arms and torso too. Her nipples beaded as small hairs stood to attention. Everything—all of her skin, all of her body—was exposed. Her clothes were gone.

Her teeth chattered and body trembled as she unsuccessfully

fought the urge to cry. This couldn't be happening. It couldn't be real.

As occurs in dim light, her eyes adjusted, allowing the prison around her to materialize.

There wasn't much to see.

The same dull white walls, four of them, created a box—perhaps more of a rectangle than a square. The ceiling was high and painted the same white as the walls, devoid of color. She searched for a light or even a bare bulb. The dim illumination that allowed her to see didn't come from electricity but from a narrow strip of glass high upon one wall. It was a window, but not one that would open. Even if it did, it was too high to reach and too small for her to fit through. As she stared, the distortions in the panes caught her attention. The glass was reinforced and leaded, the kind of window found in renovated ancient castles to keep invaders out or prisoners in.

The only interruptions in the sameness of the walls were two doorways. One was covered with a solid wooden door, closed and painted to match the monotony of the room. She didn't need to check to see if it were locked. The absence of a handle told her that it only opened from the other side. The other doorway appeared open, simply a frame with no door.

A quick flash.

She blinked.

Had she imagined it? She scanned each surface, searching for its source.

Again.

It didn't last longer than a millisecond.

Like the walls, the tiny flash was devoid of color, so quick and insignificant that if she blinked at the same second, she would have missed it. Shivering upon the makeshift bed, she waited and counted.

Twenty-two seconds.

If the room were brighter, she wouldn't have noticed it. Nevertheless, she did.

She counted again.

Twenty-two seconds later, it flashed again.

The flash came from a small knob fitted snuggly into the window sill. Well disguised, it could pass for a blemish in the trim. However, imperfections didn't flash. It was a camera and meant that she was being watched.

Another person may not have known, but Natalie grew up with surveillance as part of her life. It hadn't bothered her before. Then again, before, she'd been clothed.

It was too late to pretend she wasn't awake. Now that she was sitting up, whomever was watching already knew the truth. Her empty stomach twisted. Not whomever—Dexter. The man on the plane, in the car, and in this room. The man who undoubtedly stripped her of her clothes. The monster who stole her life. He would know that she was now awake. How long had she been asleep? Would he be coming to her? Was he asleep? What time was it?

Did she dare look in the other room?

Again, her stomach complained.

She clawed at the bed in the dimness, hoping for a blanket, sheet, or even the mattress covering, something in which to wrap her body. But there was nothing, only a metal cot with a single scratchy mattress.

Turning from the window—from the camera—Natalie used her arms and hands to cover her breasts and core. It wasn't much, as she hurried toward the open doorway. The concrete floor was cold beneath her bare feet as she rushed forward.

Once within, she fumbled along the wall for a switch and in the air for a string. Nat found none. This room was darker with no window, only the dim light trickling in from the room with the bed.

As her eyes continued to adapt, the second room came into focus: a simple yet efficient bathroom. Everything was white, reflecting light and helping her see. Straight ahead upon a pedestal was a sink, to one side, a toilet, and to the other side, an old iron clawfoot tub. Above the tub, mounted on the wall, was a showerhead. Reaching in the darkness, she searched for a curtain, one to contain the shower's spray.

Rings rattled upon a track, higher than her head, but the curtain was gone. Natalie sunk to her knees and crawled about the cold floor, searching for towels, a robe, or anything. Back on her feet, her hands splayed over the walls. An empty towel bar beside the toilet and an empty hook near the doorway were all she found.

Thankfully, there was toilet paper, but it would take the entire roll to cover her, and then what if he wouldn't replace it?

How could she even rationalize his thoughts? These were the doings of a deranged madman. She wasn't crazy. He was.

Again, her stomach grumbled.

Did he plan on starving her?

Natalie reached for the handle on the sink. Air and moisture sputtered, and then water began flowing. Using her hands, she cupped the cold liquid and brought it to her lips. The stench of sulfur filled her nose, worse than the musty aroma of her cement cell. Without drinking, she opened her hands and allowed the water to splash into the sink and disappear down the drain.

Perhaps at least, she could make it warm. That would help.

There were two handles. Natalie turned the handle on the left of the faucet as far as it would turn. As she waited for the temperature to change, she took care of other business. Her hand stilled as she began to wipe.

Had he touched her...there? Obviously, he'd taken her clothes off. Had he raped her?

Memories were fuzzy at best. She recalled floating or being carried. Though she was cold—chilled to the bone—and her muscles ached from trying to keep herself warm—too long rigid and contracted—she didn't feel injured or sullied beyond her nakedness.

When she'd boarded the plane to Munich, Natalie Rawlings had been a virgin. Surely, she'd know if she weren't any longer.

Forgetting about the camera, she carried the toilet paper into the light and sighed. There was no blood. She'd heard there would be blood.

Natalie wasn't completely without sexual knowledge. She'd dated boys in Iowa. They'd kissed and petted, but even with the biggest football star, she had a figurative wall around her, protecting her from going too far. No one dared be the boy to look her father in the eye after taking her virginity.

At Harvard, it was different, yet the same. Though Anthony Rawlings's reputation held no boundaries, it was Natalie who didn't want to cross that line. It was she who didn't want to face not only her father but also her mother, not until the man who earned her hymen was also the one who earned her heart.

Some would consider it old-fashioned.

Maybe it was seeing her parents' devotion to one another. She wanted what they had. They'd overcome more obstacles than she even knew, and through it all, they loved one another unconditionally. They had the kind of love that survived life's trials and came out stronger.

Tears returned. Will she ever see her parents again? Can

their marriage survive the tragedy of losing their daughter? Did they even know she was missing?

The ache in her chest grew larger, bubbling out with an audible sob.

Throwing the toilet paper in the water, she grabbed another piece and wiped her eyes. As it all swirled in the darkness and disappeared down the drain, she straightened her neck. She would survive this ordeal. Somehow, some way, she'd make it back to them.

Reaching for the running water, she expected heat. The reality was barely a few degrees above ice, reawakening her chill. Beside the handle was a small bar of soap. As she washed her hands, she turned off the one handle and tried the other.

A buzz or whistle sounded—shrill yet short. Had it come from the pipes? Natalie tried to listen, to hear it again. Like the light of the camera, would it recur?

With each passing second, the sound stayed away; only her beating heart thumped in her ears. However, to her delight, the water warmed. To her cooled skin, the liquid heat was heaven. On any other day, in any other place, combined with the stench, this water would be unacceptable. Today, in this hell, the slight rise in temperature was the best thing she'd found. Forgetting everything else, she stood still, allowing the warmth to run through her fingers and return her circulation. As her hands warmed, she splashed some on her face. Even though she couldn't dry it, the water took away something—cleansed her as well as restored something, bringing her back a small sense of normalcy.

When the warmth began to fade and she turned off the faucet, a shadow passed over her, chilling her skin. Was it simply a figurative cold to the loss of her warmed water? Had she imagined it?

Though there was no mirror above the sink—only more wall, the same as the rest—she lifted her face. Even without the reflection, Natalie knew. Standing taller, she braced herself as the hairs on her bare skin came to attention like small soldiers ready to fight.

What she'd endured so far was only the prelude. The battle was about to begin.

"Turn around, bug. We have rules to discuss."

CHAPTER 9

Of all the animals, man is the only one that is cruel.
He is the only one that inflicts pain for the pleasure of doing it. ~
Mark Twain

Dexter's command hung in the musty air.
     Paralyzing fear.
     Natalie had heard it mentioned in books and had seen it portrayed in movies. It was a thing of fiction until it was real...*so* real that even blinking seemed impossible. Only involuntary tasks commenced—those functions that never really stop. Her heart beat, though the rhythm was like none she'd ever known,

erratic and accelerated. Her blood continued to flow, yet did nothing to bring her warmth. Even her lungs took in breath. It was enough to keep her alive, but for how long and to endure what?

It was when her trembling from earlier returned, causing Natalie's hands to visibly shake and her knees began to knock that she managed to reach out to the sink, an anchor to keep her from falling.

"Rule number one..." His tenor slowed. "I don't repeat myself."

Natalie had never been fully nude in front of a man—even those she'd dated. She wasn't a prude; she was merely twenty.

"M-may..." Her voice cracked, the word stuck in her throat, barely a croak. She didn't know how any of this worked. She only knew she didn't want to face him, to see him, or for him to see her, not as she now was. Natalie cleared her throat, still facing the wall as her fingers gripped tighter to the edge of the sink. "Please, may I have something to wear?"

His shoes upon the cool, hard cement floor echoed, each step reverberating louder and louder against the bare walls as he came closer. When he stopped, she looked down. On either side of her bare feet were shoes—boots with rounded toes. She thought they were the same ones he'd worn on the plane, but she couldn't be sure.

His body, merely inches behind her, radiated warmth, the temperature she craved. Yet his proximity did little to reassure her.

Dexter's large hands moved up and down her bare arms, feathering her skin, a conduit of electricity springing the small hairs to life, similar to the effect of rubbing a balloon. "You're cold."

It wasn't a question. There was no sympathy to his statement. It simply was.

"Yes."

He leaned closer, near enough to touch, yet just far enough not to. His coffee-flavored breath reawakened her hunger while also caressing her neck and shoulder in warmth. "Tell me, bug, how you can get warm."

Her mind filled with possibilities, none of which she wanted to entertain. Each of his words weighed a ton until her head dropped forward, unable to bear the load. With her chin to her chest, tears filled her eyes. She answered the only way she knew how—honestly. "I-I don't know what you want."

Dexter took a step back, his boots echoing against the stark bathroom fixtures. "Rule number two, disobedience will always be punished. If I tell you to turn, turn. If I tell you to answer me, answer."

Her shoulders quaked. If there were a door on the bathroom, she'd close it. It wouldn't really be an escape, but it would give her space. And then she realized...the door. The one he entered.

Quickly she spun past him and raced forward. As soon as she neared the barrier, she saw the error of her ways and came to a stop. She was naked in the better lit room, and the door was shut, locked, still with no way to be opened. However, that couldn't be true. Dexter was with her. He wouldn't lock himself in, would he?

She closed her eyes as the tap of his boots echoed upon the concrete. Her dread grew as each step came closer and closer.

"You have a great ass," he said, running a hand over her skin. "Show me what else I want to see."

"Don't, please." Natalie pleaded, recoiling from his touch.

"You saw me—everything. You had to see. Who took off my clothes?"

He barely touched her shoulder, encouraging her to turn.

Flinching again, she spun, her loose hair landing upon her shoulders. With a steely expression, she faced him. What difference did it make? He'd obviously undressed her.

She sucked in a breath as, for the first time as his captive, Natalie truly took in her captor. This was different than on the plane or even in the airport. As they stood, Dexter Smithers towered above her. His body was bigger than she remembered —more powerful. With him in his boots and her in bare feet, everything about him made her feel small. As the seconds ticked away, she shrunk under his intense stare.

It wasn't his words or even his hands that kept her in place. It was the way he was looking at her as his nostrils flared and jaw clenched, and his blond hair fell just over his ears and near his eyes. His gaze pinned her down as the turbulent ocean-blue orbs silently roamed up and down her body. Like his touch, his scan was fire—a scalding-hot poker raking her skin.

Finally, he spoke. "Legs shoulder-width apart."

Her eyes squinted in the dim light, as if seeing him clearer would give meaning to his words. "What?"

Dexter lunged forward.

Natalie gasped.

His hard body stopped inches away from hers as her chin became locked in his iron grasp. Though she tried to pry her face from his hold, she couldn't.

Pulling her gaze to his, Dexter said, "I'm running out of patience." The ocean of his eyes was deep and murky, churning with the turbulent tenor of his commanding tone. "I've waited for this moment far longer than you can imagine. Now I've waited for you to wake. I've waited for you to turn and show me what's mine. I won't wait any longer. Don't ask me to repeat myself. You heard my instructions."

When he didn't release her chin, she slowly repositioned her feet, moving one and then the other.

"Hands at your sides, fingers out, and palms away from your thighs."

Since she had reached up to his hold upon her chin, trying unsuccessfully to loosen his grip, it took conscious effort to make her hands obey, to untangle her grasp from his, lower her arms, unfurl her fists, and turn her palms out.

"Shoulders back and breasts out." He made a show of stepping back and admiring her breasts. "I like them. They're not large, but oh, the possibilities are limitless."

Her eyes closed.

When he released her chin, it began to fall forward.

"No." He lifted it. "You're a proud woman. I don't intend to change that."

She audibly exhaled at the absurdity of his statement.

Dexter grabbed her loose hair and yanked it backward, causing her to wince. "Don't do that. Don't make assumptions. Don't assume that I'm debasing you to make you less. When this part of our journey is complete, you'll be more than you ever imagined." Releasing her hair, he took a step back.

"Before I entered this room there was a noise, a buzzing sound. Did you hear it?"

"Yes." She'd thought it was the pipes.

"When you hear that sound..." He tapped the floor with the toe of his boot. "...you'll stand here, facing the door, offering yourself." His gaze narrowed. "Do you need me to mark it with an X?"

"No." She wanted to mark him with an X—on his chest and use it as a bull's-eye.

"Day or night, it doesn't matter. This is where you'll be. You'll stand as you are right now. Legs parted so I can see your pretty pussy. Chest out, so I can watch your nipples bead. Hands at your side, surrendering yourself to me, and most importantly, your shoulders back and chin high. Do you know why?"

Her thoughts were equal parts indignation and fear. How could she possibly know why this man did or required anything? With his stare demanding an answer, a tear fell from her eye and she responded, "No."

He stepped closer, caressing her jawline as he'd done on the plane. To her cold skin it was fire. "Because you may be my bug, my Nat, but you're no one else's. You're a queen, no longer your daddy's spoiled princess. A queen who'll learn to appreciate the spoils of life. That understanding will give you a regal comprehension that others will see and respect." His smile widened, causing her empty stomach to clench and knot. "And a queen bows to only one person." He walked around her, challenging her to move from his required position. One circle and then another. Taking her in, admiring her body while wordlessly claiming ownership.

It reminded Natalie of the way her father or brother would look at a new sports car, inspecting it from every angle, knowing it was now theirs to do with as they pleased. Drive it, pamper it, or recklessly crash it and get another.

Dexter's words snapped her back to the misery of her new reality. "Tell me, my queen, to whom do you bow?"

The answer was obvious; it was right there. But Dexter Smithers wasn't her king. He never would be. Not as long as he treated her like an object, a thing to be ordered about. She may be naked in this cold room, but that didn't change who she was. She was Natalie Rawlings, and she didn't bow.

When she didn't answer, Dexter applied sudden pressure to her shoulders and pushed her down, commanding her new position. "On your knees."

Fuck you.

The words were on the tip of her tongue, which is wisely where they stayed. The floor bit into her knees. She fell forward, her hands extended to stop her face from hitting the concrete, when all at once her head was yanked back by a fistful of her hair.

"No. Get off your hands. You aren't crawling, not this time. Kneeling is like standing, only lower. You'll now assume the correct position."

The tears fell faster. "I don't know—"

Crouching down on his haunches, he secured her head back until their gazes focused upon only one another. "You will learn. Now tell me, have you knelt before another man?"

"No." The word was choked with new tears of both pain and humiliation.

"Never put a cock in your mouth?"

She shook her head to the extent she could. "No." Though more tears fell, her mind was on alert. If he made her do that, she'd bite him. It would probably end worse, but that was her plan.

"That's it, bug..." He leaned forward and kissed her cheek, tasting the salty emotion. "...you saved the tears for me." He licked his lips. "They taste better than I imagined. I'm sure I'll enjoy many more. Now, as with standing, knees spread..." He released her hair and using the toe of his boot eased her legs farther apart. "Back straight, sit back on your heels with your toes as your support."

She did as he said, and without instructions, she rested her arms at her side, opened her fists, and turned her palms up.

"Very good. Now tell me, which is a more comfortable position, standing or kneeling?"

She swallowed. "Standing. The floor is hard."

"You didn't turn when I told you to turn. Where will you be the next time I enter?"

God, she hated this man. She also hated kneeling. "I'll be standing where you said..." Her heart ached, but the words could save her this humiliation. "...how you said."

Dexter nodded. "Good girl, but no. In the future, yes, but not next time."

Her eyes opened wide.

"I promised you punishment. This is it. You'll remain as you are." He looked up at the window, at the camera. "You already know that I can watch you. Don't move, shift, or so much as readjust your pretty pink pussy. If you do, your next punishment will be worse, and the next one even worse, until it's your blood I taste instead of your tears."

Her entire body clenched. He couldn't possibly mean what he was saying. The concrete dug into her knees as her toes bent uncomfortably. She couldn't imagine staying this way. "How long?"

Her stomach again rumbled.

Instead of answering, as if spurred on by the audible sound of her hunger, Dexter smiled and stood. "I almost forgot."

The buzz filled the air as he walked behind her. She was facing the bed, but the warm air entering the room told her the door was open and that it was warmer beyond the doorway. If only she could turn and look, but just as quickly, Dexter was back, carrying a tray.

"I'd planned to discuss so much more, my expectations and rules for our relationship. I'd planned to do that over coffee and pastries. They really do make amazing baked goods here. The

Sachertorte is my favorite." He removed the cloth napkin, uncovering a tray.

The aroma of coffee and rum-infused cake replaced the musty air. Like Pavlov's dog, her mouth watered and fingers twitched.

Dexter set the tray on the bed, turned over one of the cups and poured rich, warm coffee from the decanter. Bringing the cup to his lips, he hummed. "It's too hot to drink right now, but the mug feels nice and warm." He placed the mug on the tray. The plate before her was filled with the famous Austrian cake.

Did that mean they were in Austria? Or did they serve that in Germany?

Natalie couldn't think as her lips parted in a silent plea, and her fingers ached to touch the warmth of the cup.

"I had plans, bug. Plans that you decided weren't to your liking. Plans you sabotaged by disobeying." He poured the second mug. "This would have been yours." He shrugged. "I suppose technically it still is."

Her heart raced. Yes, even coffee would help her hunger.

He placed the full mug on the tray. "Good girls get rewards. Bad girls are punished. Don't move, and don't even think about touching this tray. You didn't earn it."

The emptiness in her stomach spread to her chest, a defeat so overwhelming that she made no attempt to stop the new stream of tears. This was some sick kind of torture.

What could he do that would be worse? Whatever it was, it couldn't be as bad as starving on the cold floor, could it?

Though her body didn't move, her eyes followed his.

"Whatever you're thinking," he said, "I promise your imagination can't begin to conjure the possibilities." He leaned down and kissed the top of her hair. "Don't test me. Bugs can be squished." He ground the toe of his boot into the floor and then moved it toward her knees, spreading them even wider, exposing her core and causing her thighs to ache. "I'll be watching."

His steps reverberated through the cool air until she couldn't see him anymore. There was another buzz, a gust of warm air, and the closing of the door.

This can't be happening. This can't be real.

Her eyes closed. Perhaps she could forget about the tray, but it was impossible while the scrumptious aroma surrounded her. Seeing it within her reach was worse than not having it. With each passing minute, her toes ached more and more. Even her thighs called out in pain.

Perhaps it was hunger, perhaps the effect of the drug, but as time passed, her head began to bob, to fall forward, as her eyes fought to stay open. Each time it fell, she'd pull it back. Through it all, her neck and shoulders screamed out as muscles fought to maintain her position. No longer could she feel her extremities. The tingly sensation had passed; now there was only heavy nothingness.

Natalie didn't know how long she'd been there. There was no way to measure time.

She assessed the clues. The light through the window was now brighter. The coffee was no longer warm as no steam came from the dark, rich liquid. Though she hadn't drunk anything, her bladder again felt full.

CHAPTER 10

Have patience. All things are difficult
before they become easy. ~ Saadi

Had he expected this to be easy?

As Dexter made his way out of the concrete suite, his mind battled between anger—that things hadn't gone as he'd planned—and satisfaction—that she was now his. He had her. The months—no, years—spent bringing his plan to life had paid off.

Natalie Rawlings now belonged to him.

He hadn't known in the beginning that she was the completion of the prophecy, the one set in motion before both of their births, yet with patience and observation it became clear. How many times had he sat outside the fringe and watched her interact with others? It was via both in person and surveillance. In person had been the hardest. Not because he was concerned he'd be caught. Hell, he knew her security team by sight and that she didn't like to stay under their watchful eyes.

It had been difficult because she was there within reach, and yet he couldn't touch her.

Everything was different now.

From Natalie's interaction with her family to her friends, Dexter saw in her the qualities he wanted and needed. She wasn't like many of the other women he encountered. There was an element of submission that perhaps even Natalie didn't realize she possessed. It was in her, part of her, and he would nurture those needs.

Yes, one day she'd be his queen and his legal wife. He was certain of that.

She would also be the opposite: his slave, to command, praise, and punish.

The way he saw it, what he was giving her and would be teaching her was a gift. Natalie would learn to accept that there was no greater joy than to be everything to the man who loved her.

Certainly, she'd experienced pleasing a man.

Dexter had seen the way some of the young men at Harvard had looked at her. He'd sat a few tables away as she went on dates. Of course, he couldn't follow them back to the dorms, but he knew how young women were these days and pleasing people was in Natalie's nature.

He'd be lying if he didn't admit that it bothered him that he wouldn't be the first man to have her, but the reassurance that he would be the last was the fuel that powered his obsession.

Natalie Rawlings would kneel before him willingly, and he'd reward her submission with both pain and pleasure, the two contrasting elements that when combined were the yin and yang that they both needed. If she hadn't learned that yet, he would enjoy teaching her.

He'd been honest when he'd told her that he didn't intend to separate her from her family forever. No, one day the mighty Anthony and Claire Rawlings would happily invite him into their home and lives, where he should have already been.

His plan was perfect. Dexter had thought of everything— except the human element of incompetence. He didn't tolerate ineptitude in himself. He surely didn't accept it in others.

Diane Yates, the woman he hired to be Natalie on the plane and in the airport, the one who went through customs, performed perfectly until she didn't. Her blunder almost ruined everything.

"Herr Smithers," the house manager said, as Dexter entered the main level of the villa.

"Frau Schmitt."

"Sir, is there anything I can get you? Is everything all right?" Her words were in German, a language that Dexter had mastered years before.

Was everything all right?

The answer was yes—and no.

Dexter answered in impeccable German, speaking as a local, not the foreigner he was. "Yes, everything is all right. However, I was going to eat after I used the gym. I went downstairs and left the Sachertorte there. Bring me more to this office."

As he spoke he opened the massive door to the palatial office that was as different from Natalie's suite as night was

75

from day. Thick, rich carpets in shades of gold and red covered the floor. Stately ornate woodwork decorated the walls, surrounded the windows, and lined the bookcases. The draperies were heavy, framing the glass panes that looked out onto the snow-covered land.

His connection to this villa was rather complicated as it had belonged to his father's first wife's family. It was her last name that the locals knew. When she passed away, it went to Dexter's father. Though even her last name was Smithers when she inherited it, the nearby townspeople still referred to it as the Becker home—the Beckers had been established here for so long. The staff he employed, which was a skeleton crew compared to when his parents were alive, knew him as Smithers. It was the anonymity with others that made this the perfect location for Natalie's transition from Rawlings princess to Smithers queen.

"Yes, sir, right away. Would you also like some coffee?"

"Yes." His answer wasn't his first concern as he brought his computer to life, seeing the small image in the corner of Natalie on her knees as he'd left her. A smile came to his face.

Despite the serious fuck-up of Diane's and their resources, Natalie's family wouldn't find her, not until he was ready.

"Sir, do you want me to retrieve the tray from earlier?"

He'd made the rules to the staff clear. The lower level was his and it was off-limits. More than likely, they wouldn't find his hidden corridor behind a false panel in the well-appointed library. However, he didn't intend to take that chance.

"No. Don't bother. I'll bring it up later."

"Yes, sir."

As Frau Schmitt hurried away to fetch his food, he settled back in the large leather chair. While watching his prize, his queen, his student, Dexter dialed Diane's number on his untraceable phone.

He was calling hers, the one he'd purchased. If she knew what was good for her, she'd disposed of Natalie's phone as he'd instructed.

"Mr. Sawyer?" Dexter hadn't told Diane his real name. It was merely another step toward keeping his prize. Even a well-paid resource could become a liability.

"Diane, tell me the phone is no longer with you."

"Yes, sir, I did as you instructed. I'm so sorry that I answered. It was that it rang right after I sent the text you told me to send..."

Dexter shook his head. Incompetence. He'd already heard her excuses. He didn't have the patience to hear them again. "Have you retrieved the luggage?"

"Yes, sir, both bags."

"Dispose of the suitcases as we discussed. The contents need to be donated and distributed in the locations I gave you. Keep me abreast of your progress and your payments will appear in your account. No sooner or later. The schedule is not flexible."

"Yes, sir. I know. I have your instructions."

"Go to Zugspitze after you make the withdrawal and then wait for my call."

Without waiting for her response, Dexter disconnected the call as a knock echoed from his office door.

"Herr Smithers, I have your breakfast."

Dexter took one last look at Natalie on his screen. If the time on the clock hadn't changed, he could assume it was a still picture, not live feed. She hadn't moved.

His smile bloomed.

Her father's determination and her mother's submission.

It was the perfect combination.

His cock hardened as his mind filled with the possibilities of things he could do to his queen. Him and no one else. Soon she'd be satisfying his every desire.

Anticipation filled his circulation. The fun was about to begin, but first he'd let her endure his punishment. What he had in mind was a marathon, not a sprint. This wouldn't be the last time he punished his bug. No. He'd also reward her obedience. One day she'd beg for what only he could give to her.

Changing the screen on his computer, he readjusted himself and answered Frau Schmitt, "Come in."

Yes. Natalie wasn't the only one to be hungry. However, she was the only one who needed to wait to eat.

"Frau, have the cook complete the menu I laid out, and then the staff may be dismissed until tomorrow morning."

"Herr, we can stay."

He feigned a smile. "I'm a single man on my own. I don't need around-the-clock staffing."

"It is—"

He waved his hand. "Frau, your income will not change. Enjoy the reprieve while I'm here. I came here for solitude."

She nodded. "Thank you."

CHAPTER 11

*Some things are so unexpected
that no one is prepared for them.* ~ Leo Rosten

Natalie talked to herself throughout the punishment or whatever it was—Dexter's power trip. She didn't do it audibly: he could see her through his little blinking camera. It was possible he could also hear. Instead, she spoke in her mind. The process helped her stay awake. Fainting was always an option; it would lessen the pain from the floor and her position, but then what?

What would he do?

He'd told her not to even try to contemplate the possibilities. Truly she couldn't let her mind go there. Instead, she concentrated on what she would do.

She wouldn't faint. She wouldn't beg. She'd survive. She'd do it without giving him another reason to punish her or exert whatever power he thought he possessed. If he were cold and uncaring to her, she would be the same to him. She would fight his ice with ice, his commands head-on. Somehow she would convince him that he could trust her, and then the first time she finally found herself on the other side of the door, back in the sunlight, she'd run.

It didn't even matter where they were. No matter where he had her, what country, there had to be a US embassy. Her father was wealthy and influential. Anthony Rawlings had friends and business associates all over the world. They may not be the type of friends he invited to his home for a barbeque; nevertheless, they were the type of friends who would come when he called. Her father would move heaven and hell for her. Of that, she had no doubt.

Natalie wouldn't be forgotten or allowed to disappear simply because she supposedly decided not to join her family. No matter who that other woman was, Dexter's plan was flawed. Natalie's immediate family may be in Nice, but that didn't mean that her father didn't have connections. The abrupt change in her plans would serve as a red flag signaling her family's security—Phil's people—to track the other Natalie. Once it was discovered that the other woman was an imposter, it would be all over the international channels: Natalie Rawlings was missing.

As time passed, the pain from her position subsided until she felt nothing at all. Her extremities lost feeling, the needled sense of having fallen asleep morphing into nothing at all. To keep her mind moving, she'd contemplated her situation. In hindsight, it was clear that she'd been Dexter's target all along.

But why?

What was Dexter's motivation?

Since she was naked, sitting—no, make that kneeling—on a concrete floor in basically a dungeon, the sexual component was obvious, but there had to be more. He could have kidnapped any woman, but he didn't. He'd set his sights on her. It didn't take a genius to figure out that the *more* was money. Anthony and Claire Rawlings's daughter was a valuable commodity.

All of her life her parents had preached caution and safety. The cameras and bodyguards seemed like second nature while at the same time felt like overkill. Natalie had never in twenty years seen or felt a threat. Had there been some and Phil's team had thwarted them? Had everyone in her father's world kept the specifics away from her to protect her?

What had that false sense of security cost her?

If only she'd flown to Nice on a Rawlings plane as her mother wanted.

Her regret was stifling, compressing her soul as tears continued to flow.

Natalie recalled times when she'd pondered a life away from the watchful eyes of her father's security. It wasn't that the security bothered her. Knowing she was watched hadn't changed her plans or behavior, because it always was. Yet there'd been a part of her that longed for a simpler life than living up to the high standard set by Nichol.

Getting away from the Rawlings expectations had sounded like a dream. If this was the fulfillment of that dream, the reality was a nightmare. The realization that this was truly happening —the nudity, the stark cell, the now-cold drink and food that were forbidden yet close enough to touch—triggered more tears. Each salty droplet burnt a trail down her cheeks, dripping off her jaw and landing in a warm splash on her cold breasts. Each tear took a piece of her soul until the pieces begged for glue—for a way to come back together.

She wouldn't give up. Natalie's hope was her knowledge of and confidence in her family. The Rawlingses would never hesitate to monetarily pay for her return. It was her goal to convince Dexter that they'd pay more if she were returned unharmed—unsoiled, so to speak.

Buzz.

Natalie's chin snapped upward. Despite her crying, her tears were now mostly dry, and her nose had ceased to run. Her plan was in place. She'd had her breakdown. Now it was time to appear strong and indifferent, the same way he appeared. If Dexter wanted to believe she would play his sick game, she'd let him.

His scent reached her first, the aroma of his cologne. It brought back memories of his suit coat, the one he'd given her as a blanket in the car.

Still facing the bed and the tray of untouched food and drink, Natalie couldn't see what was happening behind her, only hear it—the tap of footsteps and swish of wheels.

Wheels? Did she hear wheels moving over the hard floor, like wheels on a cart?

If only she could turn, but she refused to give him another reason to retaliate. Instead, her mind filled with possibilities. She pictured the carts used by the staff at the estate in Iowa that brought food to the dining room or to the suites. There were the carts used in hotels when room service was summoned. Each of her thoughts had a common denominator—food.

Her stomach had surpassed grumbling, giving up as it had

grown accustomed to emptiness. That was until the new sounds revived it: a pang and softer rumble murmured in the damp, musty air.

She closed her eyes and tried to summon non-food alternatives. There were the carts the maids used at the estate as well as in hotels, ones with bedding and supplies. That possibility even excited her. A towel for the bath or a sheet for the bed. Such simple needs.

Natalie pushed down her expectations. If she didn't hope, Dexter couldn't disappoint. She feared that would be worse than more punishment.

As each second ticked by, marked by the tap of his shoes upon the concrete, she began to wonder if he planned to talk, to acknowledge her obedience—anything. The anticipation of what may occur brought her tired, aching body back to life, restoring the circulation and bringing needles to her veins. The new rush created a painful and prickling sensation.

Natalie stifled a cry, biting her lower lip, careful to stay silent and vowing to keep secret her suffering. And then Dexter changed the rules by giving her what she feared most and what she had believed was only hers to find—hope.

The door shut with a thud. Before she could fathom that he'd left her again, Natalie wobbled as an all-encompassing heat enveloped her.

His lips came close to her neck as he wrapped the blanket around her shoulders. "I'm very proud of you, my bug." He kissed her hair.

It wasn't just a blanket. It was a warm blanket like the cloths on the airplane or a garment recently removed from a heated dryer. The plush heat tingled her cold skin. The circulation that had resumed, generated by anticipation, now sprinted to life. The temperature was heaven, but the consequences were hell.

ALEATHA ROMIG

Pleasure and pain. Natalie didn't know which instigated her tears.

Dexter crouched beside her, wrapped the blanket tighter. And then with his hands on her shoulders, he asked if she could stand.

Natalie stared.

There was something different in his gaze. His eyes were lighter, his expression serene.

"Bug, answer me."

She tried to reach up, to lift even her hands. Her arms were dead weight, raising them only a few inches took all her strength. Her legs were nothing more than noodled pincushions. It was as if her bones had lost their rigidity. She shook her head. "I-I don't think so."

What would he say? Would he be upset?

Dexter nodded and stood. Her heart sank. Would he leave her there?

After removing the tray from the bed and placing it on the floor, in one swoop he reached down and lifted Natalie from the floor, pulling her into his arms as if she weighed nothing.

Nat cried out as her toes and legs exploded in pain. It was worse than any cramp or charley horse she'd ever experienced. Gritting her teeth, she buried her face against his broad chest.

She hadn't meant to find comfort in his attention, but she did. His shirt filled her senses with the memory of fresh air—clean and cool, so unlike her surroundings—while his cologne added just the right amount of musk and spice.

With her cradled in his arms, Dexter sat upon the bed.

She didn't know what to say or do. This wasn't the same man who'd made her kneel for hours on end. It was, but it wasn't. In her deprived state, her thoughts couldn't keep up.

"Tell me," Dexter said.

Natalie looked up to his face, trying to decipher the riddle. Even his tone was different. Maybe it was hunger making Natalie delusional. She couldn't be sure, but for some reason her plan of being indifferent was forgotten. She wanted to answer. "My toes..." Her eyes closed, her lashes dampened with tears. "My legs..."

"They hurt?"

Natalie nodded.

Balancing her on his lap and against his chest, Dexter reached for her foot and his large hand squeezed.

Pain shot up her leg. Natalie screamed, louder than before.

"No, bug," he said soothingly. "It'll get better. Give it a minute."

Biting her lip, she watched as he massaged one foot and then the other. As he continued to caress and apply systematic pressure, she found that he was right: the prickling subsided and before she knew it, she started feeling better.

"Remember my saying that the rush of blood to starved tissues can be more painful than the pressure?"

She nodded.

"That's what happened." He kissed her forehead. "I didn't think you'd make it. I really didn't. You're so much stronger than I realized."

His words flowed through her, providing the same effect as the blanket. She didn't want to like pleasing this man, but she did. She enjoyed this tone, the way he held her and wiped her cheeks. And then he placed her upon the edge of the mattress and stood. All at once, she was hit with the startling realization that she didn't want him to leave. She didn't want to be left alone again, even with the blanket.

"Dexter? Are you going?"

When he turned, his lips parted. There was something new

in his gaze: shock or surprise. She was too sore and hungry to understand.

He dropped to one knee and placed his hand over her blanket-covered leg. "Say that again." His command wasn't urgent, more of a request.

"I-I'm sorry if I shouldn't..." This was all so new. She didn't know what she was supposed to say.

Caressing her blanket-covered thigh, he explained, "No, just say what you said, exactly as you said it. I want to hear it again."

"Are you going?"

His head shook. "My name. You said my name."

"Dexter?"

"It's the first time you've said it."

She blinked. "It was?"

Again, his knuckle ran the length of her jaw. "Yes, bug. And I like hearing it from your lips."

"Are you leaving again?"

"No, not yet."

Unexpected relief came with his answer.

He reached for her hands. "Now can you stand?"

"I'll try."

The circulation had returned the feeling back in her legs. Gingerly, she shifted her weight to her feet and rose. Her legs quivered and her feet were heavy, but his grasp of her hands gave her the extra-needed leverage. Like a newborn deer, she stood unsteadily.

"How do you feel?" he asked.

"Sore, but I can stand."

"And walk?"

Natalie nodded.

Dexter tilted his head toward the bathroom. "Go do whatever you need to do. I'll give you privacy. When you come back out, we'll have the talk we didn't have this morning."

She tugged the blanket around her, but after only one step, she stopped. "May I..." It felt strange to ask for such a mundane thing. Dexter said they'd discuss the rules, but they hadn't. She wanted to be sure she wouldn't upset him. She'd do whatever was necessary to avoid the cement floor. "...may I keep the blanket...around me?"

He nodded. "I think for now...you earned it."

"Thank you." Nat hurried toward the bathroom as too many diverse emotions fought for supremacy.

Somehow, after everything, it was gratitude that prevailed.

Her mind told her she was being ridiculous. Grateful for a blanket? Yet she was. She could cover herself in the bathroom. She could keep it wrapped around her while they talked. Yesterday, she would have told herself it was silly to be thankful for a blanket. That was before.

Today, her life was different.

CHAPTER 12

The best way to find out if you can trust
somebody is to trust them. ~ Ernest Hemingway

Natalie came to a stop, standing unmoving in the bathroom's doorframe while contemplating the possibility that Dexter had been right threatening her with a psychiatric facility. Perhaps she was delusional. Hunger and stress can be triggering factors. Sleep deprivation is another. She'd slept, but more accurately, she'd been drugged. Wasn't that different?

"Come and sit," he said, turning and catching her stare.

Tentatively, she moved forward, the blanket snug around her.

In the brief time she'd been in the bathroom, he'd set up a small round folding table with two chairs. The cart she'd heard before was now in the room. Two covered dishes, a decanter, and a large glass bottle of water were upon it.

Natalie eased into the chair he pulled out.

"This is still," he said, pointing to the water decanter. "I can bring sparkling next time, if you prefer."

She shook her head. "I like still, thank you."

Definitely delusional, having a surreal conversation discussing water as if she weren't wearing a blanket and at Dexter's mercy.

He placed the dishes upon the table and removed the silver domes. The air filled with the most amazing aroma. The cake from earlier was gone. In its place were large grilled sandwiches, each with a side salad of leafy greens and vegetables.

Natalie's hunger came back with a vengeance, gnawing at her insides and making its presence known in audible growls.

When she began to reach for the sandwich, he stopped her. "Not yet. Patience."

Dejectedly, she placed her hand on her lap. Would he again tease her with food and then not allow her to eat?

Dexter placed a mug on the table and poured from the decanter. It wasn't the dark, rich coffee aroma she'd anticipated; instead, the liquid was lighter in color. The steam filled the air with a familiar scent. Before she could decipher the flavor, Dexter spoke.

"Ginger tea. It should help your muscles."

"Thank you." She'd been taught to be polite, but she couldn't help but think that he was responsible for her sore muscles.

Dexter took the other seat and scanned their meal. "Tell me, bug. What do you want?"

Closing her eyes, she pressed her lips together and compiled. Her list was simple and yet comprehensive: her life back, freedom, outside, her family, sunlight, clothes, a shower...

The movement of the other chair scraping over the concrete floor caused her eyes to open. Dexter was no longer across the table, he was directly in front of her, his face in hers. His jaw set. She gasped.

"Don't hesitate." His harsher tone was more commanding. "When I ask you a question, don't overthink. Answer immediately or lose the opportunity until I feel generous again." His jaw clenched before he added, "From now on, everything in your life comes through me. Don't forget."

She didn't know how she could. Taking a deep breath, she answered his first question. "To eat, please. I want to eat." It was the obtainable goal. There were bigger wishes she wanted granted, but at this second, as her hands shook with hunger, food was paramount. She scanned the table. She also wanted the ginger tea.

It had never been her favorite flavor, yet she'd read that the Chinese believed it to have healing qualities. While her legs were better, the muscles were tight. "And drink, tea...please," she added.

Slowly, his chest expanded and contracted and nostrils flared. It was obvious that he was thinking, contemplating. She just didn't know what he'd decide.

How does one predict the moves of a madman whose actions have already proven unpredictable?

"No more warnings," he said. "Keep rule number one in mind."

"You don't repeat yourself," she said, remembering his rule.

Her breathing stalled as he tugged the top of the blanket, lowering it from up around her neck, where she had the edge of the material tucked, to below her collarbone and lower still. Natalie's eyes closed. She wanted to stop him, to scream or reach up and scratch his hand, but she knew that none of that was within her power. She could do that, but it wouldn't help and most likely would result in the loss of her meal.

When she opened her eyes, in her current seated position with Dexter standing, she couldn't help but notice his arousal. As his hand lingered, her skin chilled.

His gaze swept from her chest to her face and back again. The blanket was now as low as the swell of her breasts. His warm finger traced her skin, dipping between her round globes along the hem of the blanket. She was no more exposed than she would be in a scooped blouse, yet it felt as if she were once again naked.

Dexter lifted her chin until their gazes met. His voice was raspy. "What will you do to earn your meal?"

Everything within her froze. Her blood forgot to flow.

"Please, Dexter." She purposely used his name, hoping for the effect from before. "I know that isn't an answer to your question, but I don't know what I can do." It was a truthful answer. She didn't want to offer more than he'd accept, nor did she want to offer less and lose her second chance at a meal.

Again, he traced the scoop of the blanket. "Lower it," he said. "Keep your breasts exposed for me, and then you may choose one thing from the table."

One?

Her heart sank as she scanned the feast. Sandwiches and salad weren't by definition a feast, but to her—on this day...at this odd juncture in her life—they were. What difference would it make if she removed the blanket? He'd seen her totally nude.

ALEATHA ROMIG

She took a breath. With trembling fingers, she reached for the edge of the blanket.

Her eyes focused on the plate. She didn't want one thing. She wanted it all. "One?"

"Rule number one."

Natalie nodded. He wouldn't repeat himself. He'd said *one* thing.

She wondered if she removed the entire blanket, could she earn more than one item. With a ragged breath, she opened the blanket, leaving it draped over her shoulders with her chest exposed. The cool air hardened her nipples.

A deep murmur resonated from Dexter's throat. Pushing the material over her shoulders, he left the rest bunched around her waist. "Now touch them."

Touch them?

In his tone, she heard his meaning. Dexter didn't want her to just touch them; he wanted her to touch them as she would alone in her darkened bedroom.

Again, she lifted her hands.

His eyes stayed glued to her movement as she kneaded both breasts, pushing them up and twisting her hard nipples until her breasts grew heavy and engorged. As she caressed and teased, it was impossible not to notice that his erection grew, straining against the zipper of his jeans.

How long did he expect this to go on?

Her skin warmed under her own touch and lips parted as she startled herself with a small, unexpected whimper. Was her body's response from her own ministrations or from the lustful gleam in his blue-green eyes? While his erection scared her, there was more, something new and erotic in what they were doing. A strange tenseness formed between her legs, causing her inside muscles to clench.

92

Surely, she wasn't turned on by this man.

Finally, he spoke, his voice weighted with lust. "You've earned two things from the table." He turned and went back to his chair.

Natalie let out the breath she'd been holding.

"What do you choose?" he asked

"The tea and the sandwich." She didn't hesitate, didn't overthink.

Dexter poured water for himself and nodded.

Taking that as his sign, Natalie hurriedly dove in.

Never had anything tasted as delicious. Natalie had grown up with talented and capable cooks who could make anything. Her mother was a fine cook when she chose to be. She'd eaten at some of the best restaurants with the world's most renowned chefs, and yet the sandwich in her hands surpassed all of that. The bread was heavenly, grilled to the perfect crispness. Between the slices, the vegetables were sautéed and pasted together with rich white cheese. With each bite, the flavors exploded in her mouth. The blanket he'd moved off her shoulders, fully exposing her breasts, was forgotten. Chewing and swallowing monopolized her thoughts while the added warmth of the mug gave her hands needed heat.

Dexter watched silently as she ate her sandwich and drank her ginger tea. He watched everything, not only her breasts, but also the way she sipped the tea, wiped her lips, even the way she chewed. His gaze was omnipresent. Once the sandwich was gone, he asked, "Wouldn't you like some water? It wouldn't be good for you to dehydrate. Besides, there was only one cup of tea."

Natalie did want water, but she was beginning to understand that everything came with a price. Instead of reaching for the decanter, she spoke.

"May I have water?"

He poured the clear liquid into her glass.

When she didn't reach for it, he grinned. "Good girl, bug. I was right about you. You're a quick learner. Are you ready to learn what you must do to earn that water?"

Though dread flooded her veins, the food she'd already earned gave her strength. "Yes."

"This time, your job is simple. It's not your body, although you'll soon offer me more than a view of your tits."

Offer? Did that mean he wouldn't take?

Before she could give it much thought, he told her what he wanted. "Your mind."

CHAPTER 13

It is hard to fight an enemy who has
outposts in your head. ~ Sally Kempton

"My mind?" Natalie asked.

"Tell me what I want to know, and you'll earn water. Tell me enough, and I'll even leave you the bottle. The water from the pipes isn't fit for consumption. Taking care of you is my job."

But you'll kidnap, freeze, and starve me to death? Instead of saying that, Natalie nodded.

"Go ahead," he prompted, "take a sip."

As she lifted the glass to her lips, she remembered his cocktail from the plane. She looked at Dexter's glass of water. She couldn't remember if she'd seen him drink any. Her hand stalled. "Did you...is this...?"

"Does it contain the drugs I gave you before?"

Her parched lips came together as she silently agreed.

"Will you believe me?"

It was a good question. She shouldn't. "I don't know. I suppose I have no choice."

"Yet you'd ask. You hesitated. Why?"

She did as he said, answering honestly and not overthinking her response. "Because I didn't like it. I didn't like the way it made me feel."

Dexter nodded. "That water isn't drugged. Go ahead and take a drink."

Obeying, she was rewarded with a clear, clean, and refreshing drink. Unlike what the rancid water from the pipes would have done, each swallow from the glass lubricated her tongue and throat in a way the tea hadn't. How long had it been since she'd had water? She wasn't sure how long she'd been asleep, and then there were the hours spent on the floor.

Natalie didn't want to stop drinking. Dexter had said *one* drink. Perhaps if she never stopped swallowing, it would still be one. Her mind told her to put the glass down, but she couldn't. It tasted too good. Now that her body had food, this was the other element to life.

The realization hit her: no matter how strange her life had become, she wanted life. She wanted to live.

Finally, she put the empty glass down, scared to look across the table at what she might see. Instead of anger, Dexter's laugh echoed throughout the small room, reverberating over the stark walls. "My bug was thirsty. Now then, I allowed you your reward before you did your part. It's time. Tell me what you're thinking."

"What I'm thinking?"

He moved his head back and forth. "If I wanted a parrot, I would have taken one. I took you, a thinking and breathing sexy, smart woman. I took you, bug. You're now mine. Tell me how you feel. How..." He gestured about the white room. "...this makes you feel and your thoughts from the time you woke until now."

It was a tall order. Exposing her breasts was easier than her thoughts.

Don't overthink. That was what he'd told her.

"I was scared. I still am."

"Go on."

"I was hungry. That's better." She looked around the room, suddenly realizing it resembled the images she'd conjured in her mind about foreign mental institutions. She wasn't the one who was crazy. No. That person was sitting across the table from her, his arms folded over his wide chest, assessing her and her exposed breasts. "I'm embarrassed and quite honestly, humiliated."

"Why?"

She fidgeted with the blanket on her lap. "I'm sitting here without a top, without clothes, with only a blanket. It should be rather obvious."

"You're mine. I'm keeping you. That means every part of you, bug. There's nothing that should embarrass you. Baring yourself to me shouldn't be embarrassing."

"But it is," she answered too quickly. "I don't know you, and regardless of what you say, I don't belong to you. I'm not your *bug*." Nat shook her head. "I really hate that, too. It's patronizing."

His blue-green eyes lightened with amusement. "Well, that won't stop. I like it. And as I told you, you'll earn your name back."

Earn. Why was everything earned?

"Now tell me," he went on, "what proof you need to understand that you do belong to me, that you are mine. Would a bill of sale make it better? A contract? I can have one drawn up that we'll both sign, but essentially a marriage license is the same thing. The one we have now isn't real. But one day…"

When she didn't respond, he continued, "How about my intimate knowledge of your sexy body? Will that prove that you're mine? For example, the way your pussy clenches even when you're unconscious?"

Natalie gasped, squeezing her legs together. "Did you…?"

"Did I…what? Fuck you?"

She didn't respond as tears filled her eyes. If only she could cover all of herself with the blanket, her face, her head, and of course, her breasts.

"No," Dexter answered, "I didn't. I want the first time that I'm inside you to be something we both remember. As much as I wanted to…" He uncrossed his arms as his biceps bulged, and he leaned forward. "…and I still want to—I didn't."

A lone tear trickled down her cheek. "Thank you."

More gratitude for things that should never be gifts: a blanket, food, and her purity. And then she remembered his words. "But you said you know how…how I clench?'

"One taste. I'm a man, and you're a beautiful woman who was bared to me. One day you'll want me to taste you, to bury my face in your cunt until you scream my name. It was only one taste."

Her head fell forward as more tears flowed.

"Bug?"

Her head snapped up. "Violated!"

Dexter's gaze darkened. "I didn't violate you."

"You asked me how I feel. There, that's it. Violated."

"You were not. I could have. You were right there." His large hand slapped the table. Plates and glasses jumped as silverware clanked and water sloshed. His expression hardened. "I could do it right now. Who's going to stop me? Not you. Not anyone.

"You need to get that through your head. You're now mine to do with as I want. Even knowing that you're mine—at my disposal at any time—I respected you enough to go no further than to remove your clothes, taste your lips, kiss your soft skin, and yes, take one small taste of your warm pussy.

"Do you know what you did?"

She shook her head. She didn't want to know. The meal she'd eaten along with the tea and water were churning faster by the second. "No."

"You instantly became wet. Did I want to be inside you with my fingers, tongue, or cock? Yes, but I didn't. I'm not sure what other assholes you've been with, but when I do those things, it'll be with your consent and for your pleasure."

Her neck straightened. "None." She wasn't sure why she'd told him—why it slipped out—but she had, and she couldn't take it back.

"None," Dexter repeated her word slowly as the realization hit him. "None, no one?"

She shook her head.

"You've never been with a man?" He stood, the astonishment overtaking his whole demeanor. "Answer me, damn it."

"No! No assholes in my past, no good guys either." *You're the only asshole.*

Dexter ran his hand over his face and paced a small circle.

"Fuck. Fuck." He turned her way. "No, you're lying. You're twenty years old. High school...college?"

"So because I never slept with a man, there's something wrong? Fine, there is. And I want to keep it that way." Tired of this discussion, she pulled the blanket back over her shoulders and tucked it around her chin, covering her breasts. "I'm not lying. I'm also done with the sandwich. Leave the water, if I've given you what you wanted or if you've *taken* it. If you're not satisfied, don't leave it. Let me dehydrate or starve. I don't care. Whatever. I'm done."

He yanked her to her feet, holding her shoulders at arm's length. "You're not in a position to dismiss me—ever. We're done when I say we're done." His eyes were now the deepest ocean depth. "Do not fucking lie. Are you a virgin?"

She lifted her chin. "I was when I woke yesterday."

"One fucking taste, a kiss to your sweet, wet lips. I didn't...how the fuck would I know?"

Indignation rang as her volume increased. "I don't know, you could have asked or let me tell you. There are more possibilities than drugging and kidnapping me!"

She didn't see his hand until it was too late. The slap echoed throughout the room. Her cheek stung as tears filled her eyes.

Dexter took a step back. "Don't make me do that again."

Make him? What could she possibly say? He'd just hit her, actually slapped her.

Dexter's tone hardened. "Respect. I gave it to you by not fucking you when I could—which includes right now, too. You give it to me. That was your last outburst. The next one will be met with a harsher reply."

Harsher than a slap?

She straightened her shoulders, ignoring the tears flowing down her cheeks. "Yes. I'm a virgin. And if you want the money my father will pay to get me back, you'll return me to him that way."

Dexter took another step back, increasing the distance between them and rubbing his hand over the dark blond stubble on his chin. "You have this all wrong. I'm not holding you for ransom. Not everyone is after your daddy's money. I have plenty of my own.

"You're here for one reason: because you're mine. We're meant to be together. I'm not returning you." He turned a small circle. The muscles in his neck tensed as his jaw clenched. "Now, bug, we're done. Drop the blanket."

Her eyes widened.

He tipped his head toward the floor, the spot where she'd knelt. "Stand in position—unless you'd rather kneel." His blue-green eyes shone her way, daring her to disobey.

With her heart beating faster, she dropped the blanket and made her way to where he'd pointed. Biting her lip, she did as he'd said: feet shoulder-distance apart, shoulders back, arms at her side, palms out, and lastly, chin up. The cold chill returned, tracking up her body with a prickling awareness from the soles of her feet upon the hard floor all the way to her tingling scalp.

As if she were no longer there, Dexter busied himself, putting the food back on the cart as well as the table and chairs. Once the room was clear, he turned. His gaze moved up her body, lingering momentarily on her pussy and then her breasts. When their eyes met, he said, "A virgin." He shook his head. "I guess I do know how to pick them."

Natalie momentarily closed her eyes.

"I'll leave the blanket and the rest of the water. Don't move until the door is shut. When I return be exactly as you are now. For the rest of the day, my two rules are simple. First, no touching or pleasuring yourself. Don't think that you can in the bathroom. There's a camera in there too. And do not bathe. We'll discuss that on my next visit."

He walked closer until the musk of his cologne filled her senses and the warmth radiating from his chest rippled over her bare skin. "Tell me, have you? Touched yourself? Made yourself come?"

Heat sparked in her cheeks. Not only there, a flicker of flame heated her core with an embarrassing rush of warmth.

"Please, Dexter."

His grin grew. "Oh, you have. I can tell. It's permissible to think about it. When you do, think about how much better it will be with a man, one who knows how to please you." His knuckle caressed her jaw. "That's it, bug, imagine. Just do not touch." He stepped back as his cocky grin widened. "Can you behave?"

"Yes."

"For the record, I said you should never feel embarrassed, and I meant it. I'm glad to know you've touched yourself. I can tell the idea turns you on. Your cheeks are pink, and I smell your arousal." He laughed. "Even caressing your own tits made you hot. Remember that now, even touching your own perky breasts is against the rules. I'm the only one who can bring you that kind of pleasure."

He tweaked her nipple. "Oh, the possibilities." He pinched it harder.

"Ouch," Nat said, not moving from her position.

"What I didn't say is that I wouldn't humiliate you. I will. Because I also enjoy that. I'll also exalt you. You can plan on me doing both. Just remember, it'll only be me who'll debase you, only I'll see you broken, because only I can put you back together.

"You're my bug, but more importantly, you're also my queen. No one else will ever see or know what we do alone."

Her breathing deepened at his final statement. Though his speech left her future open to more possibilities than she could conjure, his words weren't said as a threat, but as a promise.

And then he was gone. Natalie's shoulders relaxed as the door shut. She rushed to the blanket lying on the floor and wrapped it around her.

She replayed the entire encounter.

She wasn't insane or having a break with reality. Dexter was.

The man was certifiably nuts. What did he mean that she was his? What did he mean about her not being ransomed? If she weren't, how would she get back to her life? And how dare he tell her not to touch herself? She hadn't planned on it. But now, the seed was planted...

CHAPTER 14

We must accept finite disappointment,
but never lose infinite hope. ~ Martin Luther King, Jr.

The Rawlings family listened to Phil through the telephone's speaker. His explanations and revelations regarding Natalie's strange text message and subsequent messages did little to relieve their anxiety.

"She didn't disappear into thin air!" Tony's deep voice resonated as his statement was punctuated by the pounding of his fist on the antique desk. Normal reasoning had been lost days ago. A wizard in all things business, Anthony Rawlings could be ruthless. His family, however, was another matter. They were his salvation, his joy, his world. The deep lines emanating from the sides of his dark eyes as well as dark circles below were but outward evidence of the sleepless nights since their family holiday was derailed.

Claire's face fell forward at the sound of her husband's frustration. Each piece of unrest added to the stress. Her emerald green eyes were bloodshot from crying too many tears, yet they hadn't seemed to dry out. As the family looked closer at the computer screen, more moisture teetered upon her swollen lids. Taking a deep breath, she too focused on the image.

"These are the photos from the Munich airport in customs," Phil said through the speaker. He and Taylor had flown immediately to Germany to track down the missing Rawlings princess. "With the holiday, it's been difficult to get cooperation. Finally, I involved the US Department of State. Even with them, half the workforce is unavailable, on holiday themselves. The problem is that Natalie is an adult. We have no proof of foul play. According to her messages, she's simply missing the planned stay in Nice."

As Phil spoke, repeating the excuse they'd heard from every public agency they'd contacted, Claire stared at an ever-changing slide show of grainy black and white pictures. According to German customs, this was the footage that showed Natalie's entrance into Munich. In each shot, her head was down.

The hairs on Claire's neck stood to attention. This was the first time they'd seen the pictures.

"As you can see, that's the backpack she always carries when she travels," Phil said.

Claire shook her head. "Something isn't right."

"...no issues with the border patrol..." Phil continued to speak.

Claire knew her daughter and even with the poor quality of the photos, she was certain that wasn't her daughter.

"That's not her," Claire said, speaking louder.

Everyone in the room turned her direction. There were only two eyes she saw. The room grew quiet until Phil spoke again.

"It's difficult to see with the quality of image, but these are from the German border patrol, with the help of the US embassy. They were able to trace her back from her passport."

Claire shook her head as Nichol wrapped her arm around her mother's shoulders. "Mom, we can't really see her."

"Tony, that isn't her."

He looked from his wife to the screen. "Stop the slide show," he said. "Go back."

Slowly the pictures showed in reverse order.

"Stop."

It was a rare look at the young woman's face.

"Goddamn it!" Tony said as he turned back to Claire. "You're right."

Slowly all four sets of eyes took a step closer.

The image on the screen enlarged. Again, it was Phil speaking. "I think you're right. I'm sorry. I was going with the information..."

"What does this mean?" Nate asked. "Does that mean someone else had her passport? Did she ever get on the plane? If that's not her, where is she?" His concern was evident in the way his deep voice pitched higher with each question.

"Do you have any images of the plane disembarking?" Tony asked.

"Yes," Claire said, a small kernel of hope coming to life. "Let me see everyone getting off that plane. I don't care if she's been disguised. I'll know her."

"Phil?" Nichol asked, "what about the text messages?"

"They're now coming from a new phone. Nat's phone was found at the airport. I wish that were a good thing."

"Why isn't it?" Claire asked.

"It was left on. Natalie would know we'd find it."

"So it was done on purpose. Couldn't she have done it?" Nichol asked. "I mean, maybe she wanted you to find it, to know she was avoiding you."

"Phil," Claire spoke without acknowledging their older daughter. "In the text messages I've asked her personal questions, as you suggested, and she's answered them." She reached out to her husband's extended hand. "It has to be her. She has to be..." Claire couldn't get herself to say the word *alive*. She refused to believe there was any other possibility.

"Even though the location is turned off, Taylor and I have been able to triangulate the origins of the texts to a wide geographical area. If she would call and speak for any length of time, we'd have a better chance of pinpointing her location."

"I've tried to call back," Claire said.

"We all have," Tony said.

"The phone is turned off, immediately going to no voicemail. I know," Phil said a mask of professionalism hiding the combination of grief shrouded with annoyance. It wasn't like him to run up against brick walls. Claire knew he was as upset at himself as he was at Natalie.

"Phil, don't give up, please," Claire said.

"Roach, we know you've got this. I don't give a damn that we don't have proof that she didn't do this willingly, but I think there's more. I think..." He hesitated as he looked toward his wife. "...we need to at least consider that she was taken."

Claire saw the conflict in her husband's handsome features. "Taken?" she repeated, goose bumps dotting her skin as the dam inside her mind burst, flooding her thoughts with suppressed memories.

"Claire," Phil said through the speaker, "Taylor and I have been discussing the same possibility. I wasn't going to say anything until I had more."

"The pictures of the passengers?" Claire said, searching for a way to help Natalie. "Get me the pictures and then we'll be sure she made the flight. If she didn't, she's still in the United States." Her voice grew higher. "I'll go back today. If she's there, I'll be there."

"I'll go," Nate volunteered.

"No," Tony said. "No one else is leaving. We're all staying together. Eric flew back to the States. John is there. If we need anything there, one or both of them can handle it."

Phil spoke again. "I'll get the manifest and any surveillance from the boarding and debarking as soon as I can. The timing couldn't be worse. With the holiday, no one is on the job. Whether it's US or German agencies, or the airlines, everyone is operating with crews of temporary or part-time workers. No one knows what he or she is doing, much less who I need to speak to. Getting answers is worse than pulling teeth."

Claire took a deep breath as she sat. "It's been three days since I spoke to her. Christmas…"

Tony turned to his wife. "Our daughter will be with us by Christmas." His tone left no room for disagreement. "She is just ashamed of failing at Harvard. She was embarrassed. We need to let her know that doesn't matter."

Tony had known about Natalie's grades and decision not to pursue tutoring or remedial assistance. He'd learned when the payment for her next semester had been returned to his bank account. He'd considered speaking to her about it long distance. He and Claire had even talked about flying to Boston, but they both decided that Natalie would tell them when she was ready. They assumed that it would be during this trip. They weren't happy, but it didn't qualify as something warranting this type of behavior. Never had they devalued their daughter's ambition or achievements in any way. They were waiting to hear her explanation and learn her future plans. No matter what they would have been, Tony and Claire would have supported Nat.

They knew that. It was difficult to believe that Natalie didn't.

Nichol let out a sigh at her mother's statement, as she too sat on a sofa opposite her mother.

The rest of the family turned to her.

"Fine," Nichol said, her hands in the air. "I'll say it. Everyone is thinking it. I'll be the one who rips off the Band-Aid. Natalie is spoiled. She always has been. She's throwing a temper tantrum so that when she shows up on Christmas Eve or Christmas morning, you'll be so happy that you won't get upset about Harvard. If this was a kidnapping, don't you think we'd have heard something by now? Some demand?"

"We're not ruling anything out," Phil's voice transcended the miles, the voice of reason that he'd been for as long as Claire could remember.

"Good," Claire said, standing and staring at her oldest. "You're wrong. Natalie wouldn't do this. She wouldn't. I don't care about Harvard, and for your information, your father and I already knew. We were waiting for her to tell us. Besides..." The tears were back. "This is your baby sister."

Nichol stood too facing her mother. "Mom, I know. I just think that it helps you rationalize her behavior if you think she was taken, but she is a Rawlings. Something you and Dad have told us all forever: a Rawlings can't be taken without anyone noticing."

"We are noticing. And yes, she is a Rawlings and worth a fortune to us."

"Then why haven't you received demands? Why have you only received her *I'm going to find myself* text messages? Maybe because that is really what happened; she's pouting at some expensive hotel in Germany or Sweden or resting by a warm fire with some hot guy buying her drinks."

"Nichol." Tony's one word received the room's attention. "If you were missing—"

"She isn't missing, Dad. She's texting."

"If you were avoiding us, doing something completely out of character, we would want to learn why and make sure you were safe."

"I wouldn't."

Claire's neck straightened. "Neither would Nat."

Nate cleared his throat and took a step toward his dad. "We'll pursue both options?"

"Yes," Tony said. "I'm tired of the dead ends. I don't give a damn if she's an adult. We're involving all the governmental authorities. No media. I don't want this made into a public spectacle with a million false sightings. It's time to bring her home."

Sitting back on the sofa, Claire closed her eyes as a dull ache pounded behind her temples. She liked the tone of Tony's voice. This was the man in charge, the one who would bring their baby back. She needed to trust in him as she had always done.

Her mind slipped back to years, decades before. A dew of perspiration covered her flesh as horrors she'd willed away bubbled to the surface. Claire recalled the terror of awakening in a strange bedroom. Her stomach twisted with the rekindling of fear, the knowledge that she was a prisoner...that she was at the mercy of...

When her eyes opened, the same dark eyes were right before her. Tony was kneeling by her legs with his large hand on her knee. His thumb gently wiped away a lone tear that had escaped from her eye.

"Don't, please," his deep voice held more emotion than he often showed, even to his children. "She is safe."

"But...I know what it's like..."

"That isn't happening."

The fact that both Nichol and Nate knew their parents' history allowed Claire to express her concern without the need for explanation. Though they'd kept it from Natalie, their baby, Nichol was older. At too young of an age, she'd been exposed to a web post that she was never meant to read. And then, one night in a fit of rage at her parents, she told her brother. It wasn't the type of memories a family discussed over Easter ham, but nevertheless, it was their history.

"I can't help but worry...I can't help remembering."

Nichol sat down beside her mother. "The texts say she's off on her own, thinking. That's where she is. History isn't repeating itself."

It was strange how they could all refer to that tragic time with no more than a wistful sigh.

Claire reached for Tony's hand as she leaned against Nichol. Nate took a step closer and reached for her other hand. "I love you," she said. "All of you." She nodded at her children and also toward the screen, where Phil's image now showed. "I'm scared for her." The words rang true in a way that only one who has also suffered the unimaginable can recite. Yet, as Claire stared from one face to another, even into Tony's regretful gaze, she knew she wouldn't change her past. It brought her the present.

She also didn't want her daughter to experience anything similar.

Nichol's reasoning was harsh, yet it made sense. However, if Nat were off pouting at a ski resort, why did Claire's stomach twist with dread.

"Have there been any indications of her using her credit cards?" Claire asked.

"In the airport in Germany. She bought two disposable phones and a bottle of water," Phil answered.

"See?" Nichol said. "She's all right."

"How did she get where she was going? What about a hotel. It's been three days."

"Any charges since then?" Nate asked.

"A cash withdrawal of 1000 euros."

Nichol forced a smile and nodded.

"What about a picture from the ATM?" Tony asked.

"It's grainy and with the cap, you can't see her face."

Claire sighed as Tony helped her stand. "Please, Phil, find her. Bring her home. We don't care about Harvard. She has her whole life in front of her. Please bring her home."

"What if you stopped her credit cards?" Nate asked.

"No," Tony replied.

"I agree," Phil said. "The activity is helping us track her."

"Roach," Tony said, "Let us know when you get the other pictures. We know this woman who went through customs wasn't Natalie. Now we also need to know where that woman is and why she had Nat's information. Did she abandon Nat's phone or was that Nat? We need answers. We need them—"

"Three days ago," Claire said, finishing Tony's sentence.

They all looked toward the live transmission of Phil Roach. Since his hair had always been white, it wasn't as easy to see the aging that had occurred over time. Truly after Taylor came into his life, he seemed to grow younger, not older. His hazel eyes glistened with genuine concern for the Rawlings family. The Rawlings were his employers, but more importantly, they were his and Taylor's family.

"We won't stop. Try to get some rest. Taylor and I will find her."

"Thank you, Phil," Nate said, disconnecting the call. "You know," he said turning back to the room, "I've never seen Phil fail. We don't know where Nat is now, but we will." He again reached for his mom's hand. "She'll be back."

Claire feigned a smile. "You're right."

"Phil won't disappoint us," Tony confirmed.

CHAPTER 15

Your intellect may be confused,
but your emotions will never lie to you. ~ Roger Ebert

Days lost meaning as time passed into weeks. If Natalie were a missing person, she hadn't heard. She hadn't heard anything about anything, except from Dexter.

She'd boarded the plane in Boston on a Friday in mid-December. It had been before Christmas and her sister's birthday. She'd tried to keep track of time, but days and nights intertwined. Sometimes when Dexter arrived with breakfast, it was still dark through the small window. Some days it never seemed to get fully light. Other times, their day would end, and the light would persist.

After a few days, she earned artificial lighting. At first, she hadn't seen the source. It was a rope-type light hidden high above in the seam between the wall and ceiling that only Dexter could control. Though the room was still stark, the light helped her spirit.

Everything in Natalie's life came with a price, the value determined by Dexter. Whether it was towels for the bathroom, washcloths, sheets, or even a pillow for the bed, only he could assign their worth. Sometimes it was an act of submission or obedience. Other times, a thought or a feeling, verbally shared. Sometimes it was memories, specific questions about subjects she often wondered how he knew about.

She could question him—it was an option—but like the positive items she earned, questioning Dexter also received reinforcement—the negative kind. Questions by him were to be met with truthful answers, not more questions. Nevertheless, there were times when Natalie would purposely opt for his punishment. Accepting the sting of his belt was at times easier than recalling memories. To talk about her family and her life before while enduring her new existence was at times too much for her to bear. The bruises upon her skin would heal. The raw emotion of her wasted life and abandoned family kept her awake for hours.

While it could be perceived otherwise, everything was Natalie's choice. She could opt not to give the price Dexter determined. Which did she want: the reward or the punishment? In all things, the final decision was hers.

A mortifying change in Natalie's life was bathing. Due to Dexter's rule about self-gratification, when she first arrived, taking a bath wasn't allowed to be done in private. It wasn't enough that she knew Dexter could watch via camera: he insisted on being present. At first, he physically bathed her as if she were a toddler in need of assistance. When it was his hand that wielded the soft sponge or cloth, she was rewarded with rich-smelling bath salts, soaps, shampoo, and conditioner. And then after he'd dry her—all of her—he'd instruct her to lie on the mattress and he'd cover her skin in velvety lotions. The scents varied, but their presence permeated the musty air, creating a pleasant cloud.

Though Dexter claimed she was his, that she belonged to him, Natalie didn't really know him. His touch made her uneasy. Subconsciously, she'd tense.

Nothing remained subconscious—nothing. Dexter required her thoughts and feelings on everything he did, that she made him do, and on every reward or punishment.

"Tell me how it felt when I slapped you."

"It hurt." The answer was honest and not overthought.

"No, bug." Dexter touched her chest, the spot between her breasts where her heart resided, not the one that pumped blood, but the metaphoric one that controlled emotion. "How did it *feel?*"

The talking was worse than the actions.

It was one thing to be made to stand in a corner for hours, like a rebellious child. It was another to describe the humiliation. It was one thing to be required to crawl to his feet and sit like a pet between his knees, another to admit that the shame made her wet.

Without a mirror, she couldn't see her face, but she could see the bruises that often discolored her skin. The first one he'd given her, on her thigh, had faded, but others had taken its place. Some were felt more than seen, such as those that sometimes made sitting difficult. Others resulted from restraints or the hard floor.

After Natalie confessed that she didn't like being bathed, Dexter stopped. Since he'd listened, she should have been happy. Yet she wasn't. From that moment forward, the soap he brought to her each day for her bath was abrasive and strong-smelling. The water without the bath salts reeked of sulfur and dried her skin. The shampoo barely lathered, and of course, the lotions ceased to appear. Natalie was now free to bathe herself —with his supervision—but her honesty came with a price.

Though she now had items, like sheets, blankets, and towels, they all lacked one thing—color. The only tint outside shades of white in her world came from Dexter: his sparkling eyes, his jeans—black or blue, the color of his shirts. It fascinated her each time he entered the room. Such as the black and white photographs with one red flower or blue umbrella, Dexter's rainbow of hues became her focus. She'd watch his every move, as long as she was positioned in a way that she could see.

The day he wore a green shirt, she dreamt of the fields in Iowa. A blue one would remind her of the sky on a clear summer's day. Even black held meaning—a contrast to the white of her room.

Over the weeks, Natalie's life became a predictable routine. Sometimes she'd wake before Dexter arrived with her break-fast, other times she was asleep. No matter, she quickly learned the sound of his arrival, and after a few slow-to-rise mornings that resulted in his desired punishment, Natalie always stood as she'd been instructed, presenting herself for his entry.

After breakfast was exercise time. There weren't many options in a 12-by-8-foot room. Dexter's requirement was that she continued to move. Walk, dance, run in place, do jumping jacks, or sit-ups, the choice was hers, but standing still or sitting or lying upon the bed—the only furniture that remained permanently in her room—was forbidden. This activity continued nonstop and lasted until he arrived with her lunch. Though she had no way to tell the time, she knew it varied. Some days, exercise went on and on until continuing to pace took the last of her energy.

Meals were earned, never to be expected. Usually she sat with Dexter at the small table. Sometimes she was permitted the covering of her blanket, other times not. If he were feeling particularly dominant, she ate on the floor, kneeling at his feet, her food coming from his fingers. She soon learned that the number of chairs at the table was the deciding factor. As she stood in his desired position, her breathing would quicken if the door shut with only one chair in place.

It meant that her walking for that part of the day was done. On all fours with her breasts swinging, she'd approach his feet.

Between lunch and dinner was what Dexter referred to as *his time*. It was when Natalie's job—her ability to earn a reward —was contingent upon his pleasure and often her humiliation. He'd remind her that only he could do these things to her, only he could mark her skin and debase her. The world would see her as his queen, but first, she needed to please her king.

As the weeks passed, her virginity stayed intact.

It wasn't that he didn't touch her; he did. His fingers and hands roamed her face, neck, and collarbone. She'd stand or lie —whatever position he requested—as her breasts, tummy, and behind were pleased or punished. He saw all of her, yet he never breached her vagina.

The inattention to that particular area, combined with his actions and dominating presence, awakened her arousal, creating a desire for things she'd never before considered. Erotic, sensual needs monopolized her thoughts.

Where at first she'd thought of her parents and family, over time, it happened less and less. It wasn't because she didn't care about them, but that they lost their relevance. Dexter was in control of every facet of her life.

He was her god and her devil. His presence and approval infiltrated even her dreams.

At night, her hands would ache to give herself relief. When he'd first forbidden her self-pleasure, she'd thought it would be the easiest rule to keep. Now, it was nearly impossible. There were even times that she'd fidget against the rough sheets allowing them to abrade her hard nipples. It was when her hands wandered in her sleep that she'd quickly awaken and move them within sight of the cameras, scared that with merely one rub of her clit, she'd lose the bedding she'd earned.

Masturbating had never dwelled within her thoughts, but when she was alone with the memories of his most recent *Dexter-time*, the need was almost too great not to face. She recalled the way her hands had been outstretched and tied to the bed's metal frame. How her knees were bent beneath her and a bar had been positioned, attached to her ankles and also bound to the bed. How he'd verbally described his view.

Tears dampened her pillow at the memory. It was mortifying enough to know she'd been on display, her ass in the air and her most private parts exposed, but when that was accompanied by her own body's betrayal, a glistening essence leaking down her thighs, it added to her agony.

Bathing was next on the schedule after *Dexter-time* and then dinner.

After dinner, there were minutes or hours before the lights went out. That time was spent either alone or in Dexter's presence. That was up to him, his schedule, and his responsibilities.

Natalie didn't know what he did when he wasn't with her.

She knew nothing about anything beyond the door. All that could be seen from her designated place, the place where she was to stand when he entered or exited—assuming she wasn't bound or being punished—was a gray hallway, the opposite wall made of concrete blocks.

Wherever Dexter went or whatever he did, he was clean and smelled of fresh air and dominating spicy musk whenever he entered her room. Wherever he spent his time away from her, it wasn't in a dingy cement room. Despite the things he did to her, she found herself missing him when he was gone. Maybe his threat had been right, the one in the airport in Munich about her sanity. Maybe she was insane. Who would actually want this man's presence?

Yet loneliness was a nasty enemy. It gnawed at her thoughts like a starved rodent. While with Dexter, her mind was filled with him. His actions dominated her body and her thoughts. The anticipation of his next move kept her on alert. Rarely could she calculate his plans, yet there were signs she'd learned to read that gave her a welcome sense of predictability.

If Natalie had crawled to her meal, she could be assured that he would test her tolerance during his *Dexter-time.* While that expectedness would have been unimaginable before her life with him, in some ways she now found it comforting. It was when they sat and conversed like a normal couple consuming a shared meal that she found herself anxious and distressed. Though she knew better than to show it outwardly, inwardly she was on hyperalert.

The gallant even humorous man could almost make her forget that she was his prisoner. His aqua eyes could sparkle as he listened to her speak. His laugh filled her cell with the carefree joviality it usually lacked. During those times, even the lighting seemed brighter. Yet it could all change in the blink of an eye. It was the glimpses into the kind man who Dexter was capable of being that made his brutal reality more frightening.

As much as his different personalities stressed her nerves, when he was gone and she was alone, Natalie was worse. Yes, her skin didn't bruise. She didn't cry out with pain. She didn't break down with humiliation. However, when she was alone, she had time to think. She had time to reflect, to question, and to regret.

Her arousal at his arrival was more than sexual; it was genuine happiness to be freed from the prison of her lonely cell. It was relief that only Dexter could provide.

The only true measure of time came with Natalie's period. She'd always been regular: every four weeks like clockwork. Telling him wasn't necessary: she'd awakened with the realization.

Of all the humiliations she'd endured at his hands, this wasn't one. While she anticipated perhaps his anger over the soiled sheets and even demoralizing words, she hadn't expected what she instead received: his understanding. Feminine hygiene products appeared and her schedule lightened. Natalie wanted to tell him that she wasn't ill. It wasn't like needing a pass to be excused from gym class. Yet the reprieve was welcome.

His only demand was that she inform him when it was complete.

Like the fleeting peeks into his softer self, the amnesty was only temporary.

Her period had ended over a week ago, and now lunch was done. Since her return to their regular schedule, *Dexter-time* had taken on new vigor, as if during the reprieve he'd conjured new ways to let her earn the kindness he'd already paid to her.

It didn't make sense to want him with her. Natalie knew what Dexter would do—maybe not exactly, but she knew he would abuse her body and test her limits. She could anticipate expressing anything from whimpers to incoherent screams as she worked to endure the pain. She also knew that once he was satisfied, he'd make it better.

He'd explained that it was his responsibility to take care of her. That was why he fed her and met her needs. She was his—his queen. He would take what he wanted because he was the king, but at the same time, he'd always give her what she needed.

CHAPTER 16

*Our prime purpose in life is to help others. And if you can't help them,
at least don't hurt them.* ~ Dalai Lama

Taylor Roach watched the young woman from afar. Though the woman across the cafe resembled Natalie Rawlings, that was the extent of it. She wasn't her twin. She was at least two inches shorter and she always wore her hair in the same ponytail. She was attractive, but didn't have the beauty of Tony and Claire's daughter. All three of their children were beautiful or handsome, but there was innocence about Natalie, a naiveté that radiated from her like an aura.

If Taylor were to be reflective, Natalie had possessed that quality all of her life. And then there was her flair.

Taylor recalled Nat's creativity and style. Her hair and clothes were always changing, reflecting her mercurial personality. Some days she even changed them five or six times. Taylor and Phil would joke that she wasn't even aware that she did it, but they saw it as her unspoken barometer. Taylor couldn't recall Nat ever wearing the same hairstyle for weeks on end or the same style of jeans and sweaters as this woman did.

The woman lifted her gaze toward Taylor and nodded as she slipped the small recently purchased cell phone into the rubbish container.

Taylor waited until the woman exited the cafe before following her onto the street.

With the late winter breeze whipping their hair in knots, Taylor met her eye-to-eye and asked, "Do you have your instructions for the next text?"

"No," Diane said. "But I've been giving this a lot of thought, and I think I need to stop. I'll tell him and you that I quit."

Taylor smiled as Phil came up beside her.

"And lose your double pay?" Phil's hazel eyes squinted. "I'd give that more thought if I were you. I mean, you still have the debt that got you into this in the first place. And your sister isn't getting any better."

Diane shook her head. "But Mr. Sawyer made it clear that I couldn't tell anyone about this. He said if I did...you don't understand. He's—"

"Intimidating," Taylor said, interrupting the speech she'd heard too many times. "As we mentioned, our employer is also intimidating."

Phil grinned. "Yes, my money is on ours. And once we find

yours, he won't stand a chance. And you can stop with the 'Mr. Sawyer.' We know that's an alias."

Diane shook her head. "Listen, I don't know anything. It's the only name he's given me. I just answered an ad."

"We've heard it all before," Phil said. "Don't worry about it. Keep making the text messages he tells you to make. At this point, the people to whom you're sending them know that it's not their daughter texting. They also know we're zeroing in on her location."

"I didn't have anything to do with her disappearance."

Taylor tilted her head. "Diane, that isn't true. You didn't take her, but you pretended to be her. You lied to the German border patrol. You're not innocent."

"But I never even saw her. I was farther back in the plane. He told me what clothes to wear, and the flight attendant brought me her bag with the identification. I saw her picture on the driver's license, that's all. Mr. Sawyer—or whomever he is— didn't even want me to see him. I couldn't tell you what he looks like."

"Well, here's the deal," Phil said. "Either you keep working both sides of this charade—"

"Think of it as if you're a double agent," Taylor offered with a smile.

"Or we turn you over to the authorities for aiding and abetting in the kidnapping of Natalie Rawlings," Phil continued. "Then, not only will you be busy explaining how you had nothing to do with her disappearance, but your employer will learn that you failed in your assignment. He will learn that you've been receiving additional money. Your sister won't have your help while you're being held..." He scrunched his nose as he looked at his wife. "Hmm. What do you think? What should Diane do?"

Taylor shrugged. "I suppose it depends on how intimidating this man really is."

Diane's phone rang.

Phil and Taylor pulled out their phones, the ones with the ability to trace a call on a phone that is close enough in proximity to be connected. Phil handed Diane the same cord he'd given her at least a half dozen times. The routine was simple now that they'd figured out Diane's employer's pattern.

He gave instructions, with specifics on what was to be texted and when. The messages were being sent from every two to every five days. After the instructions, she would be told where to buy a phone. It wasn't to be bought until the morning of the text. Then after the text was sent, the phone was to be disposed of. Roughly ten minutes later, he'd call.

What Phil and Taylor wanted Diane to do was to keep this man on the line long enough to trace his location. The data they received would be stored within their phones, and then once they were connected to the laptops in their hotel suite, the search would commence.

As it was, they had him traced to Austria, south of Salzburg. Unfortunately, the elevations and terrain didn't aid in their search. Cell towers weren't nicely spaced as they would be in New York or Los Angeles. Instead, his call came from a satellite phone, its signal pinging off of reflectors currently in a heavenly orbit.

That was why they hadn't been able to track him more precisely. Each call, each additional minute Diane kept him talking, helped their cause.

"...I understand. How will I...?" she spoke with her head down, keeping the wind away from the transmitter. "Milan? As in Italy? No, I don't know another..."

Phil shook his head at his wife.

Taylor agreed. They'd been on this wild-goose chase for too long as it was. 'Mr. Sawyer' had it appear as though Natalie was traveling all over the European continent. According to the text messages and emails—which began to arrive a few days after her disappearance—she was.

At first the Roaches and Rawlings wanted to believe that the emails were actually from Natalie. Her credit cards showed activity in the areas where she claimed to be visiting. It wasn't until they located Diane that they learned that she had the credit cards in her possession.

Though Diane didn't know anything about the emails, they always originated from her location. It wasn't a difficult trick. With a VPN (Virtual Private Network) set up in each location, the origination of the email could easily be disguised. Mr. Rawlings had done the same thing years ago, making Claire's emails appear to have originated from Atlanta when in fact he had her laptop in Iowa.

Nevertheless, it made logical sense to assume that Natalie was wherever the calls from 'Mr. Sawyer' were originating. It was also the content of Natalie's responses to very specific questions that gave them all hope. She was the only one who would know the particular information she replied. It was too random to be common knowledge.

Taylor and Phil had a decent description of the man orchestrating this charade. They'd seen him on the grainy photos from the airport in Munich. He was tall, blonde, and according to his passport, twenty-six years of age. It took much longer than they wanted, but eventually it was discovered that they entered Munich as Jonas D. and Nellie Smithers.

They were currently gathering as much information as they could on Jonas D. Smithers. However, since Natalie's name wasn't Nellie, there was the possibility that Jonas wasn't his.

"...yes, sir. I promise. My sister..." Diane's voice cracked. "The doctors say if she gets the needed treatment... Yes... Thank you." She nodded. "Goodbye."

Diane looked up at the Roaches. "He always does that. Just like you do."

"What?" Taylor asked, though she suspected that she knew.

"Asks about Jenny." Tears filled her eyes. "That's why I agreed to this—she is why."

Taylor nodded supportively. "We know. That's why we're letting you help us. It will help her."

"But I can't...I can't keep traveling all over. She's home in Minnesota." Immediately her eyes opened. "Shit. I shouldn't have said—"

"Diane, we know your sister is at Mayo. Knowing things and learning things is what we do. Our employer is ensuring that her bills are paid—for now. He's making sure she is safe. Now you have to help us do the same for Natalie."

Diane sniffled her tears as she unplugged her phone from theirs. "I hope this helps you. I have to go to Italy."

"*We* do," Taylor said.

When Diane looked up, she smiled. "I guess this is better than traveling alone. I know that technically I'm alone."

"You help us," Phil said, "and we'll help you."

She nodded and handed Phil the piece of paper she'd jotted notes on while speaking to Mr. Sawyer.

He took a photo of the notes.

"Five days this time," he said with more than a hint of audible disappointment.

Taylor shook her head. "Are you making that call, or am I?"

"I guess it will be me."

Taylor was relieved. She knew Phil felt the same way, but it was hard to continually give the Rawlings incomplete reports.

This man—Mr. Sawyer or Smithers—was good. Whatever he was doing, it was clear that this wasn't random. He'd had it planned, all the way to his remote location.

Phil handed Diane the third phone she'd held in less than an hour. "Get rid of the last one. Just like always, our numbers are in there. Don't call anyone else on this phone. If anything changes, happens, or you need help, call us. And when you get your reservations, text all the information. We'll arrive in Italy at the same time."

She looked up at them. "Will you please tell her parents that I'm sorry? I didn't know. I wish I would have done this all differently."

"Yes," Taylor said. Sensing that Diane needed a friend, she reached out her hand. "You're helping now. Just don't stop."

"Okay."

CHAPTER 17

Once you consent to some concession, you can never cancel it
and put things back the way they are. ~ Howard Hughes

E ach day during *Dexter-time*, Natalie fidgeted more, craving the violation she'd previously feared. That feeling occurred at other times of the day and night, but as his strong hands moved over her exposed skin, the need grew until her desire consumed her thoughts.

One afternoon, with Natalie bent over the foot of her bed, the metal frame bruising her hip bones, and her face upon the mattress, Dexter ran his hand over her behind. His large palm warmed her skin as his touch roamed and teased the edges of her desire. He came so close, yet didn't breach her core. The thoughts of what could be if he did breach it surpassed her concerns regarding whatever he had planned and why she was in this position.

It was his touch and attention that she longed for, craved, and also feared. The combination created was a concoction continually swirling through her subconscious, its poison even infiltrating her consciousness. Whether it was right or wrong, she wanted more.

Nat adjusted her footing and spread her legs, gaining stability while wordlessly granting Dexter access. If she didn't have to admit her need—if he took instead of asked—she could enjoy it without guilt.

Her ass, legs, breasts...he never hesitated to pinch or nip, to caress or kiss. Natalie belonged to him. She was his to do with however he desired. While her mind filled with thoughts of what his fingers could do, the air split open with the whistle of a crop. She hadn't seen him bring the implement into the room. If she had, she wouldn't have been daydreaming about his touch.

The sound occurred only a split-second before the sting of the contact. There wasn't time for her to prepare. Shocked, Nat screamed out at the unexpected assault as she fought against the restraints. Whatever part of her body she could move, she did. Her legs stiffened and fists balled. Yet it gave her no relief. She was bound in place. Her sobs bubbled to the surface as the sensation continued its reign of terror on her skin and beyond.

"No, bug, internalize. Just listen to my voice."

She did, allowing the deep timbre to dominate her thoughts while he dominated her body.

His hand again roamed her skin. "It's beautiful the way the

leather marks you. It makes me happy. Do you want me to stop?"

"No," she replied without overthinking. If she thought about it, she'd want him to stop. The pain the crop brought on was sharp and unrelenting. It didn't end after the leather blade assaulted her skin. Instead, it spiderwebbed like broken glass throughout her nervous system.

Again, he teased the edge of her core. "Don't lie to me. You know how I feel about telling the truth in everything. I'm being truthful with you. Your ass is spectacular with angry red welts. Give me the same respect."

Her legs shifted at his touch as he teased the raised skin. Fighting to speak through the tears, her words stuttered. "I-I'm not lying, Dexter. You didn't ask if it h-hurt. It does." She sniffled against the blanket. "You asked if I wanted you to stop. I don't. I want you to mark me."

"Why?"

The sensation had dulled as her legs relaxed. "Because it makes you happy."

"And you'll willingly do this for me?"

"Yes." More tears came with the truthful answer.

"Ask for it, bug."

He often made her beg for things. It was humiliating and yet, stimulating. Her insides pinched as she formed the words. "Please, Dexter, mark me again."

"How many?"

It was an awful question. Nat could say it was up to him—defer it to him—but she didn't know if she could take the number he might decide. Too few and he'd be disappointed. Too many and she may not survive. He'd never broken her skin, only marred it. She didn't know how far he'd go. "Five."

Dexter's hand warmed and teased approvingly. "My brave bug. Count for me."

She again concentrated on his deep tone, allowing it to fill her. As she did, she had the sensation of swimming naked in the sound of his satisfaction and appreciation. The warm, sparkling pool took away the pain and replaced it with triumph.

If taking five strikes would please him, she could do it. "Yes, my king."

He leaned close to her ear. "We'll start at number one."

Her eyes fluttered shut as her imagined mirage evaporated. The reality ached in her chest. The one strike she'd already endured wouldn't count.

"Yes, my—"

Whistle.

Crack.

Fire.

"O-one." It took all her strength to articulate the number.

Again.

"Two."

Three blows came in rapid succession. Their point of contact crisscrossing her ass and dragging over her upper thighs.

"Three." The word came on the exhale.

The speed at which he delivered the strikes didn't give her time to think or react. Not consciously. Unconsciously, her body melted to his desire. Her rigid stance after the first unexpected strike continued to morph. Though each blow was like adding hot coals to already burnt skin and the pain grew, radiating throughout her body, she conversely found an island of peace.

Her fists released the blankets which they had been holding.

No longer perched up on the balls of her feet and toes, her tension eased, allowing her to settle and relish the coolness of the concrete. Instead of the strikes, she concentrated on the numbers. They dominated her mind. No longer only audible, she saw each digit as if it were right in front of her. Each one became a real entity, a trophy in her hands, taking her one step closer to the end.

Most importantly, each one made Dexter happy.

By the time Natalie uttered the number five, her body was numb, floating again in the warm pool of her imagination. The hot lava from before had cooled. Natalie's mind was doused in the drenching satisfaction that she'd completed the task.

Dexter's lips started at her neck and rained downward, coating her collarbone, back, ass, and thighs in his kisses, soft and gentle. His approval radiated from his touch. She pushed toward him, wanting more, as his fingers roamed, reading her raised skin as if it were a love letter written in Braille. She savored the sensation as his touch examined each mark. The inward pleasure caused her pussy to grow wetter. Ashamedly, she knew that even before the first strike of the crop she'd been soaked.

It was as he discovered the evidence on her thighs that he wordlessly acknowledged it. Spreading her legs wider, swipe by swipe, he coated her essence like salve over her welted flesh.

As the endorphins faded, Natalie's bewilderment grew. It always did. Her mind told her that this was wrong, yet her body craved Dexter's approval. All of her life she'd tried to please other people. Her choices brought others happiness. While she knew that this was similar, there was a striking dissimilarity. She also enjoyed his treatment in a way she knew she shouldn't. She couldn't even hide her reaction, not with the way Dexter coated her skin with her own cum. She was aroused.

Natalie whimpered against the soft bedcovering as he

continued to tease and roam near her core. Tears of unsatisfied need pooled upon the comforter. She gasped for breath, her dissatisfaction coming as a sob.

"Talk to me, bug. Was it too much?"

Sometimes it was easier to talk when he had her in these positions. She couldn't see his deep-ocean eyes or decipher his thoughts. She was free to talk without witnessing the consequences. "No. That's not it."

"Then to what do we owe these tears?"

"Dexter." She said his name so he would receive a response, acknowledgment that she was listening. Yet she didn't know how to answer.

"Tell me what you're feeling."

It was one of his questions that she detested. Instead of answering the way she always did, admitting her pain or embarrassment, she threw caution to the wind. "I'm frustrated and confused."

His hand stilled on her sore ass. "About?"

She shifted her footing. "Me. I don't know what to think or do." When he didn't respond, she added, "I've never felt this way before."

"This way?" It was Dexter's turn to parrot.

Her core clenched. "I need...I want to come."

This wasn't right. He'd just beaten her with a crop for no other reason than he wanted to see the marks. She shouldn't be aroused, yet she was. This wasn't a man she should want, but she did. With each strike of the crop he wielded, she lost herself in the sensation. She couldn't deny it if she wanted to. Her traitorous body had already left the evidence on her thighs.

"You want to come?"

Natalie was a virgin, not a nun. She knew the relief brought on by an orgasm. The thought alone made her clench as her nipples grew hard.

"Please." Though her cheeks caught fire with her confession, there was also relief. She needed more.

"How?" he asked.

"How?" Her pulse thundered through her veins so loudly she could hear it swishing in her ears. Was he going to grant her this pleasure?

Dexter leaned near to her tearstained face. "How do you want to come? My fingers, tongue, or cock?"

The latter scared her, but the first two sounded doable. He's kissed and licked the rest of her body. Though when she first arrived she hadn't liked it, now she did. It meant the pain was over, and he was making it better.

Natalie swallowed and stared into his turbulent eyes. The waters were rough. Would she survive the storm? She didn't know. Either way, it was time to face it. "I'll consent to your wishes, my king. And there's one other thing..." Her heart raced.

"Tell me."

"When it's time...will you..." The words were hard to say, to admit, yet they were sincere. She wanted him to be pleased with her. She also longed for the scents and colors that would accompany her request.

"Bug, will I what? Will I hurt you?"

Her ass and thighs simmered with the fire from the sharp leather crop. Later, if he'd let her, she'd touch the raised skin with the tips of her fingers. It was something he sometimes allowed, letting her, too, also admire his marks. Yet, despite her current position, for some reason, asking him if he'd hurt her never crossed her mind. Nat shook her head. "No, Dexter. I trust you to do what's best, to do what I need. I was wondering if from now on, you'd help me bathe."

A deep sound resonated from his throat. She didn't know if it was a yes or a no. She'd wait. Without answering, he reached for the restraints binding her wrists, the ones holding her down to the bed. He unbuckled one and then the other.

Though the pressure of the bed frame against her hips lessened, Natalie didn't pull away or stand. She lay as she'd been told to do, waiting for his next instruction.

Her mind was consumed with her confession of need. Dexter took care of her. He had since she met him. She had faith he would again. Her thoughts were so overwhelming that she was no longer aware of her sore ass or thighs, his marks temporarily forgotten. She'd remember them again when she was alone and hurting. But now, her king was with her.

The anticipation of what he would do—could do—tingled her body and tantalized her mind.

Natalie was his puppet, a marionette, slumped lifeless in its case, waiting for the puppet master to give her what she needed to move and come to life.

When Dexter reached for her hand, taking her palm in his, Natalie's heart thumped to a new beat. In his eyes was the mirrored anticipation that she felt coursing through her circulation.

Nat's fingers clung to his as she waited to learn the direction that he'd pull her strings.

CHAPTER 18

People grow through experience if they meet life honestly and courageously.
This is how character is built. ~ Eleanor Roosevelt

"Tilt your head back."

Natalie did as Dexter said, supporting herself with her arms as warm, clear water flowed over her hair. Coconut permeated the air, surrounding them in the scent of sunshine as Dexter retrieved another pan of water from the sink.

She watched as he stood, turning his back toward her.

With his shirt off to keep it from getting wet, she watched

the only part of his body she'd seen without clothes: his wide chest, toned back, thick muscular arms, and defined torso. She'd been nude ever since she arrived, and yet she'd never seen more of him than what she could see now. The disparity suddenly filled her thoughts.

She'd never seen any man naked. She'd seen pictures, but never of an erection. She'd felt his against her, through his jeans. Natalie knew how hard Dexter could become when he rubbed himself over her, but through the rough denim, she couldn't gauge anything else.

It had been over two weeks since she'd asked him to let her come. By the time it happened, she'd done more than ask. Her body and words begged for relief.

At first, he'd used his mouth. She would say it was his tongue, but as the memories tightened her core, she knew it was more. With her positioned over his face, he described his view. If he'd meant to embarrass her, it hadn't worked. Instead, his words turned her on, primed and ready for what would come next.

But she wasn't ready.

What Dexter did with his mouth lifted her higher than anything she'd ever done to herself. Sucking and nipping, he'd worked her into a frenzy until she was no longer conscious of her actions. Holding the headboard, she writhed as her hips rocked and breasts heaved. The tension within her built until she was sure something inside her would snap. She'd never been wound so tightly. Just as she thought it would happen— that her orgasm was imminent—Dexter told her to stop, that they were done.

Stop? She could barely comprehend his command.

She didn't want to stop. Her body begged to disobey. She'd willingly take his punishment, if she could just have more of what his mouth could provide. The scene came back.

With her knees on either side of his face, she stared down into his eyes. His lips glistened with her essence as her pussy hovered inches from his chin.

"You heard me. Don't make me repeat it."

If he repeated himself, she would be punished. But she wasn't thinking straight. "Please, Dexter. I-I'm so close."

His shiny lips smiled as his eyes twinkled. "I know. I think you can wait a little longer."

Her entire body trembled with need. "I can't."

His large hands splayed over her hips as he lifted her off him and onto the bed.

"Did I...?" She didn't know how this worked. He'd been the one to direct her position. Maybe she was supposed to have done something else. "Did I do something wrong?"

"No, bug." He kissed her cheek, leaving her own scent on her skin. "You're perfect."

"Then what happened?"

"It's time for your bath."

Her bath? Now?

Submerged in the sweet scent of lavender, he offered her the relief she'd wanted. The price was her speech. She needed to tell him how it felt to ride his mouth, how his tongue, lips, and teeth had felt on her core. And how it made her feel when it ended without resolution.

Natalie's description was simplistic and honest. It felt good and when he stopped, she was heartbroken. She'd never wanted anything more.

"And now, do you still want to come?"

"Yes," she answered too quickly without waiting for him to tell her the price. She knew she'd pay whatever he asked. "I'll do anything."

His grin widened. "Anything is a big promise."

Her breasts heaved in the warm water. It was the first sweet-smelling bath she'd had in a month. The water was even warmer as the silky salts coated her skin. "Anything," she repeated.

Dexter took her hand and helped her stand. In the clawfoot tub, she was nearly his height, but not quite. Doing as he led, she stepped to the floor and stood with her hands on the side of the tub with her back toward him. Scented water slid from her skin, pooling near her feet.

Even the cool air didn't dampen the heat of his touch as his fingers roamed her body, tweaking her nipples and moving down to her need.

Natalie shifted as the pressure within her rekindled, stronger than before.

"Talk to me," he commanded.

"Please, Dexter, touch me."

His lips found her neck as his warm breath flittered over her wet skin. "Don't let go of the tub."

She nodded. Words had become difficult to form. His kisses continued stoking the flames of the fire inside her. Through his jeans, his erection pressed against her behind. Over and over his lips roamed. No longer foreign, they left a trail of hot coals as she craved more of his touch.

When his nips became bites, her whimpers turned to moans until she screamed out, "Please..."

"Who do you belong to, Nat?"

He'd said her name. It was almost too much.

"You," she panted. "I'm all yours."

"Who's your king?"

"You, Dexter."

"Who do you kneel for?"

"Only you."

Her legs shook as his fingers found her folds. She gasped as one, and then two digits slid inside her. Just as she had with his mouth, she rode his hand, bouncing on the balls of her feet to the rhythm he estab-

lished. Curling his fingers, he stoked the fire he'd started, fanning the flames hotter than before. It was as he found her clit that his deep voice confirmed her answer, guaranteeing her release.

"Mine, you're my Natalie."

The world spun as she cried out. Fireworks detonated as relief exploded through her system. The pleasure was so intense that it teetered on pain. Her fingers blanched as she rode out the orgasm, her skin covered in perspiration as she came harder than she ever had. Her swollen clit ached as her insides spasmed. Her legs quivered and face finally fell forward. And then his hands were gone. The sound of his zipper brought her back to reality.

Her breath caught in her chest. Now that she'd come, the idea of him being inside her was terrifying. Yet she'd promised anything.

"Dexter?"

Her hands trembled on the edge of the tub.

"Don't turn around."

She closed her eyes, accepting the inevitable. He'd given her what she wanted; now it was time to pay. What was about to happen was the value written on the price tag she'd been too anxious to read.

As she braced herself for his cock, the bathroom filled with Dexter's baritone moans echoing off the stark furnishings. They rumbled through her as his breathing hastened. Yet he wasn't inside her.

Natalie longed to turn around, to see what she only heard. Her mind filled with the erotic image of him pumping his erection. She was certain that was what she heard, and then a deep roar vibrated off the walls as warm liquid splashed over her ass and back. It continued as the warmth dripped down her legs.

Nearly two months ago, Natalie had tensed at his touch. Now his cum coated her skin and all she could do was imagine what it would be like to have seen his hard cock. And then the sound of his zipper signaled the end of his pleasure.

"Give me your hand."

He hadn't told her to turn around, so she didn't. She lifted her right hand as he directed her back into the tub.

"One more time," Dexter said, telling Natalie to lean her head back as he again poured warm water. The memories of that day made her nipples bead as she concentrated on the muscles in his arms, the way they flexed as he rinsed the conditioner from her hair.

In her old life, she had her hair trimmed every six weeks. It was overdue, but Dexter liked the way it flowed over her shoulders. Sometimes he'd even braid it. The first time he'd done it, she found the attention intimate. Now when he did it, as with the placing of only one chair, the action frightened and shockingly excited her. It signaled the beginning of a particularly taxing *Dexter-time*, one that would leave her skin moist with perspiration and possibly bruised.

Today's *Dexter-time* had been a braid day. After he'd secured the end, he directed her to the bed. Like a lamb off to slaughter, she willingly obeyed. Whatever he had planned wouldn't be as bad as it could be if she fought. She'd learned that lesson early in their relationship.

It was funny that in her thoughts she described what they had that way—a relationship. That reasoning helped her cope with the reality.

Once her hands were bound above her head, he removed clamps from his pocket and showed them to her. Lying in the palm of his hand, the shiny silver contraptions looked innocent enough, but she knew the truth.

"Nipples or clit?" he asked.

Her pulse increased. She'd never had a clamp on her clit. What would that feel like? How badly would it hurt when he placed it, and worse, when he removed it?

Dexter's head shook. "You had a choice."

"Nipples," she answered.

He kissed her nose. "You hesitated. You were overthinking. Tell me what you were thinking." As he spoke he tweaked her nipples, twisting and teasing as they morphed to hard points.

"I was thinking..." It was hard to concentrate on her words as he worked her body, kissing and sucking. "...about what you said...about the blood coming back."

"How painful it can be?"

"Yes. I don't want...I don't want..." Her eyes fluttered as her breasts became heavy with need. "...you to use the clamps anywhere."

"But I do, bug." He hadn't used her name since that one afternoon. "And it's all about pleasing me. You know that I enjoy your pain as much as your pleasure."

She tugged again on her wrist restraints. It wasn't like she thought she had a choice.

He continued to tantalize her skin, elongating her nipples. His teeth nipped at the sensitive skin as he continued to talk. "Tell me again, do you not want to please me?"

Natalie swam in his voice. "I do."

"You said you didn't want me to use the clamps. I want to watch as they pinch your skin. Do you not want that?"

"I do."

"Are you sure?"

She was lost to this man. "Please, Dexter, use the clamps."

"Bug, you can do better than that."

Her body writhed in the restraints. "Please, I'm begging you."

"That's my good girl..." His voice faded as he guided the clamp over her nipple.

"Oh...ouch...." She bit her lip to keep her words from spilling out as she worked to do as he'd taught her—to internalize. Tears filled her eyes as he tightened the clamp around one engorged nipple.

"That's it." He leaned down and kissed the tear away. "Your tears are nearly as sweet as your pussy." He secured the second clamp.

Natalie found that if she ignored the pressure, concentrated on something else, the initial pain would subside...it would be bearable...until he removed them. He spread her legs, tightening her insides. Maybe he'd let her come. She could concentrate on that.

"No!" Her hips bucked and screams echoed as the clamp tightened over her clit.

Dexter's lips kissed her folds. "You hesitated. You lost your choice."

And then his fingers were inside her, working her pussy, bringing more circulation to her clit. The closer the orgasm, the more painful the third clamp became.

How could something feel so good and hurt so much?

"Please, Dexter, don't make me come."

"But you like to come. Don't hold back, bug. Let me hear your pain and pleasure."

Even in the tub, the memory brought moisture back to between her legs. She'd come harder than she ever remembered. And then Dexter ran his hands over her wet breasts, causing her to flinch and bringing her back to the coconut-scented relief.

"Are they still sore?" he asked, pinching the bruised nipple.

"Yes," she whimpered.

"How's your clit?"

"It still hurts too." She couldn't believe how easily it had become to talk to him, to answer his questions.

"Tell me your thoughts."

"Before I was remembering what we did today, I was thinking about the time you came behind me."

His eyes widened. "You were?"

She nodded.

"Go on."

"You've let me come so many times since then, yet you only did that one time. Can I...?" She suddenly felt unsure.

"Can you what?"

"Can I help you?"

She waited and watched. Though his eyes grew a deeper shade of ocean blue, Dexter didn't answer. She'd almost forgotten her offer by the time he helped her from the tub, tenderly dried her body, and after directing her to the mattress, coated her skin with lotion. Lost in the scent of sunshine, she became transfixed on the man above her. With each aromatic application, his muscled torso flexed, making the indentations of his abs more defined. His large hands—the ones that could bring both pain and pleasure—gently caressed her tender body. At times like this, witnessing his restrained power, Natalie understood what his words never uttered: it took more strength for him to control his actions than to wield a crop or cause her tears.

There was something in that realization: the knowledge that she could give him an outlet for both, taking his bite and allowing him to make it better with a kiss, caused her heart to swell. Maybe she was going crazy.

"How, bug?"

Dexter didn't need to say more. She knew what he was asking. How was she willing to help him?

"I've never seen a man...I know we're going to have sex. I think I'm ready, but first, can I touch it?"

"So only your hands?"

She shrugged. "And maybe my mouth."

Dexter groaned. "It's time for your dinner."

"Maybe this once, we can eat later?"

He stood. "Off the bed, Nat. Kneel for your king."

CHAPTER 19

Being deeply loved by someone gives you strength,
while loving someone deeply gives you courage. ~ Lao Tzu

Natalie scurried from the bed to the floor. The anticipation building inside her camouflaged the hard surface beneath her knees. She didn't notice the concrete as her breasts heaved and she assumed the position he'd taught her long ago: sitting back on her bent toes with her hands at her side.

And then her concentration was on Dexter.

Had she given up hope of ever leaving this room? She

didn't know. What Natalie had come to realize was that her life as she had known it no longer existed. The turmoil over classes and meeting everyone else's expectations was a thing of the past. Keeping up appearances and pleasing everyone didn't matter. Those pressures had been chains holding her in a box designed by her birth, family, and social status. As strange as her existence was now, it was simpler and surprisingly freer.

Natalie now had one priority. He was currently observing her every move.

Her breath stilled as Dexter walked around her, once and then again. The tap of his boots on the concrete became the rhythm of her pulse, slow and methodical, giving her strength to continue. Dexter gathered her damp hair and with a tie secured it into a ponytail at the top of her head.

Natalie exhaled. He hadn't braided it.

Again, he was in front of her. "Go ahead, open my jeans."

She reached up, and as she unsnapped his jeans, her tongue darted to her suddenly dry lips. Everything about this was scary and exciting. Through veiled lashes she looked up at her king as she reached for the zipper. When he nodded, she lowered it. Beneath his jeans, his briefs were black and silky. The hard bulge she'd only felt was now pushing against the soft material.

"Keep going."

Her throat dried as she tugged his jeans to his thighs. She'd never before so much as seen his thighs. They were defined and muscular. Did all men's thighs look as powerful? Her heart raced at new speed as she reached for the band of his briefs. His erection was in front of her, covered for only a moment longer. What would it look like?

Dexter stopped her hands. "Nat, I'm going to come, either in your mouth or on you. Do you realize that?"

With her heart thumping, she nodded. "I want you to. I want to be the one who makes that happen, like you are for me."

"Fuck," he breathed the word more than he said it.

With more confidence than she truly felt, she lowered the band. Her eyes opened wide as his penis sprang forward. Natalie gasped. "It's so big." Truly she had nothing to compare it to. She looked up to his deep, turbulent eyes. "I-I...inside me?"

Dexter petted her hair. "Not today, bug. Today, kiss it."

Surely he could hear her heart beating, the way it was pounding in her chest. She leaned forward, familiarizing herself with the only man to have her. His musky scent, the way the flesh of his thick shaft stretched, revealing veins. His hair—there—was coarse. Her lips came forward and puckered as they contacted the tight skin. Despite its hardness, the surface was velvety soft.

"Now your hands."

It took both of them as she wrapped her fingers around him. Beneath her grasp his cock thickened, growing even larger. The tip glistened as pre-cum leaked from a slit.

Up and down, her hands moved, faster and faster. More cum oozed down his cock, creating a slick medium that allowed her hands to slide as she pumped.

"Suck it, bug."

She opened her lips wide and pushed her tongue to the base of her mouth. Keeping her hands around the length, she lowered her mouth until she couldn't take any more. The flavor was musky and salty, like nothing she'd tasted.

"Fuck, that feels so good."

It was the encouragement she needed. She was doing this. Sucking his cock was like accepting his pain. It was what he expected, but unlike his pain, this didn't hurt. It was empowering.

Until it wasn't.

Dexter's hand found the ponytail he'd styled. Gripping it tighter, he dictated the movement of her head. No longer in control, Nat fought the urge to gag as his length reached the back of her throat. Her eyes watered and nostrils flared. It wasn't the same kind of pain as that brought on by a crop to her sensitive skin, yet it created the same fear. Would she survive?

Though she was unsure of what was about to happen, she didn't fight his direction. Instead, she submitted to his desire as her skin prickled, jaw ached, and lungs fought for air. She was at his mercy, and then he released her briefly, only to begin again. Soon they fell into a rhythm allowing her to breathe. As he pumped faster and faster, she forgot the ache of her jaw. No longer was she sucking; she simply existed as a channel for his pleasure. The realization dampened her core. His grip upon her hair tightened until all at once his breathing quickened, and his thrusts became more forceful and erratic.

Like other times with Dexter, this would leave Nat bruised. It wasn't something she questioned. She'd take whatever he offered—his wrath or his cum—if it made him happy. And then it happened: warm liquid spurted in her mouth. Her bruised lips tightened around his penis. There was so much of it as his cock shuddered, and more and more filled her mouth.

"Swallow."

Of course, she obeyed.

It took conscious effort to allow the first swallow of the thick, warm liquid to be consumed, but once she did, she didn't hesitate. It wasn't bad. It wasn't good, but she liked the way he possessively gripped her hair. She knew that she was pleasing him, and that was all that mattered. Gulp after gulp, she continued until all that remained was his still-hard cock.

He pulled it back.

Her eyes were filled with tears, yet her shoulders were straight.

"Fuck, Nat, that was fantastic."

Her battered lips smiled.

Dexter helped her stand. Her toes were tingly, yet she hadn't been aware of anything but him. He pulled her close as his lips found hers. A kiss, a real kiss. His tongue gently teased her lips.

He'd kissed her many times—her skin, her hair, her tears. This was different. They were kissing each other.

Natalie moaned and her core pinched as her body melted toward his. How had she not realized how perfectly they fit together? Like two pieces of a puzzle, she was where she belonged in his embrace. Craving everything about him, as his cock probed her stomach, she pushed back.

Finally, Dexter took a step away and reached for his shirt.

Her heart sank, knowing he was going to leave her alone.

She wanted to ask when he'd be back, if he was getting her dinner, if she'd done okay. But she knew the routine. Dejectedly, she turned toward the door and took her position.

His shirt came over her shoulders, hanging to her thighs. He eased her arms through the sleeves and rolled them up. Button by button, he closed the front.

Dexter smiled. "That looks good on you."

It was better than any ball gown she'd ever worn and more precious than anything she'd ever possessed. "I-I may wear it?"

He nodded with a grin. "Yes, bug, you may wear it. I'll be back."

Though he left her alone, her heart swelled as his fragrance remained.

The days and weeks that followed blended together. She'd had another period. That was her most accurate tell of time.

Dexter-time changed. Not only did he explore her body, but she also explored his. There was still both pleasure and pain, yet she was allowed to touch him as they talked more. No longer only answering his questions, she also conversed with him. She discussed her life, regrets, and dreams with him. They even laughed. One afternoon while straddling his hips, Natalie ran her hands over his firm chest. The beat of his heart thudded under her palms as her core clenched at the sensation of his erection nudging her behind.

Nat looked him in the eye. "I'm ready."

No longer turbulent, his eyes glistened like the rays of sun over the ocean's waters. "Once we do this, there's no going back."

"I know."

"You said you were waiting."

Nat nodded. "I was waiting until the man who earned my body also held my heart."

"And..."

"And, Dexter, I'm yours. You have all of me. That means my heart too. You've had all of my body except my virginity. Like the rest of me, it belongs to you too." Her face flushed. "I mean, it's up to you, but if you want it, it's yours."

His neck and chest flexed as he leaned up until their lips met. And then he lifted her off him and onto the mattress. As he stood, he reached for his jeans.

Natalie's heart clenched. "A-are you leaving?"

He handed her his shirt—the one she now wore as a dress. "No, Nat, you're not losing your virginity in this room. I took your innocence here; your gift deserves more."

Suddenly faint, she could barely breathe as her circulation quickened. "You're going to let me leave?"

"Bug, you're never leaving me. I'm never leaving you." He caressed her jaw as she buttoned the shirt. "I'm going to take you upstairs to a real bed. It's time to remember how a princess lives, but now you're no longer a spoiled princess. You've come a long way, my queen."

He reached for her hand while at the same time he pushed something in his pocket. The buzz sounded and door opened. Her bare feet barely kept up as he tugged her down the concrete block hallway. "There's no one else here now, so no one will see you."

Others? There had been other people in this house, or whatever it was? She'd never heard anyone. Had they heard her screams?

At the end of the concrete block hallway was a door. Even if she'd gotten out of the room, she would have needed another key to exit the hallway. When the door opened, she had the sensation of a movie her mother loved. Suddenly, she was Dorothy opening the door of her small home to the magical world of Oz. No longer black and white, everything had color. So much color.

Ornate carpets and rich textures replaced the yellow brick road. Her feet stilled upon the soft, plush surface. There were lush leather sofas, bookshelves filled with colorful spines of books, and a wall of electronics. The lights cast a golden hue over the deep mahogany woodwork.

It was sensory overload as he led her through the large house. It seemed as big as her home in Iowa, but they weren't in Iowa. On the first floor, she gasped at the windows—real windows revealing the world he'd kept hidden from her. Though the sun was setting, she squinted. The scene beyond the glass panes was brighter than anything she'd been exposed to in months. Reflecting the rays of auburn sunshine was a thick blanket of white. It covered everything—large trees and open lawns—like the inside of a snow globe.

Though there wasn't any snow floating through the air, she had the sensation that someone had just shaken her world.

Nat wanted to ask where they were, but it was all too much.

Step by step, she followed as Dexter led her up a grand staircase to the second floor. His large hand holding tightly to hers gave her the strength to keep moving. No longer damp and cold, the air was fresh and warm. The floor beneath their feet wasn't concrete but polished wood.

Dexter opened a tall wooden door at the end of one hallway to a sitting room. A fire simmered in a fireplace, its warmth rippling the room with heat. A few steps farther and he opened the second door. Natalie's feet stalled as her blood stilled.

Vibrant colors filled her vision, the bed covered with fluffy down-filled satin comforters. More ornate rugs and grand furniture. Her eyes roamed, knowing that this was where it would happen—where she would be forever changed. It was a bedroom easily four times the size of the room where she had been held. Heck, her room was about the size of the giant bed.

"Dexter?"

He dropped her hand and began to undo the buttons on the front of her shirt. "Natalie, I've waited for this."

She swallowed and nodded, finding comfort in his determination and patience. He had waited. This was her decision.

Dexter leaned down, kissing her hair, neck, collarbone, and breasts.

Lost in the sensations that only he could give her, Nat's eyes closed as his lips sent electricity straight to her core. And then he stopped. When her eyes opened, he was on his knees.

"Natalie, you're my queen."

"Dexter?" She didn't know what to do. It felt wrong to have him kneel. That was her job.

He brought her hand to his lips. "You're everything I've ever imagined. You said that I have your heart. Natalie, you have mine. You've had it since before we met."

"I don't understand."

"I know you don't. Just remember that I love you—not despite everything, but because of everything. That's why what we're about to do is right. It's always been right."

"You love me?"

"Forever and always." He stood, scooping her into his arms, and carried her toward the bed.

Before he set her down, she reached up and wrapped her arms around his neck. "I'm scared." He'd made her give him her mind and honesty. It only seemed right now.

"I know, bug. I know. This isn't about pain."

"But you like that."

He nodded. "I do. I also like bringing you pleasure."

After a long kiss, Dexter threw back the blankets, revealing softer sheets than she'd slept on in months. He gently laid her on the bed.

Their eyes stayed fixed on one another as he removed his clothes. She marveled at his body, that this handsome, powerful man was the man who loved her. The hardness of his muscles and the gleam of his gaze mesmerized her. By the time he climbed onto the bed, her desire almost exceeded her fear.

Dexter removed the shirt from her shoulders. Moving slowly, tentatively, he touched and caressed her folds and clit, his teeth nipping her skin until her wanton need surpassed reservation. Her breasts heaved as he finally eased over her.

And then with his rigid cock teasing her entrance, he stilled.

"Dexter?"

"I'm never letting you go."

She shifted her hips, ready for him to take her. "Please, Dexter."

"What, my little bug?"

"Please, never let me go...I don't know what I'd do without you."

"That's one lesson you don't need to learn."

She sighed as her hips continued to fidget in anticipation. "I'm all yours. Please take me." Her back arched as he worked inside her tight channel. And then as she grew accustomed to the pressure, he gave one hard thrust. Natalie cried out as pain overtook the pleasure.

"Nat, that was it." His voice was tender, soothing. "Relax, let me make it better." He kissed away her tears.

Natalie tried to do as he said—to relax. She trusted him to do as he promised and make it better. That was what he did. Whether it was her aching legs from kneeling, sore ass after a spanking, or her nipples after the clamps, he made everything better.

In and out, he moved. The pain disappeared as her body came to life.

Grasping the soft sheets as the pleasure built, she called out the name of the only man to have all of her. Dexter Smithers was the only man to give her everything she never knew she wanted. With their bodies now one, they climbed higher and higher until together they shattered, and he filled both her body and her heart to overflowing.

CHAPTER 20

Just when I think I have learned the way to live,
life changes. ~ Hugh Prather

Natalie's prison cell changed, but not her routine. Dexter's suite was now where she lived. Since the outer sitting room required clothes, he had an entire wardrobe delivered. It seemed unnecessary. There were more clothes than she'd wear in a semester—when she used to go to classes, events, and parties. There were sweaters, coats, and boots, yet she hadn't been outside since she arrived. Her world was limited to Dexter and the occasional staff member. The latter was the reason for clothes.

Dexter no longer delivered her meals, though he was usually present when they arrived. There were multiple household staff who came and went, all speaking German. They always spoke respectfully, addressing her as Frau Natalie. As Dexter's queen, she was the woman of the house. If they questioned why she rarely left the suite, she wasn't aware of it. Though over time she learned a few words of German, to explain how she'd come to live in this exquisite villa high in the mountains in Austria was impossible. She couldn't even come up with that story in English.

Behind the second door, in the room with the large bed, Dexter's shirts were all she was allowed to wear. The wardrobe he'd purchased included lingerie in all colors, textures, and lengths. Those were worn only upon request and usually meant the night would involve very little sleep. Truthfully, Nat didn't mind; it changed up her routine. And no matter how Dexter would elicit her tears, pleasure was always within reach.

There was another room attached to the master suite that contained exercise equipment. Instead of jogging in place, she now had a treadmill and weight machines. There was always something to keep her busy and her mind focused on him. That didn't mean she didn't think about the life she once had—about her family. She did. There'd been times she hadn't loved her life as the Rawlings princess, but now that it was gone, she had mixed feelings.

Though her calendar was still her menstruation chart, she knew she'd missed so much. December was more than Christmas in the Rawlings household. Their holiday would have included celebrating Nichol's birthday and the anniversary of her parents' first wedding, as well as Christmas.

February was both her father's and brother's birthdays. Her mom liked to plan something special. If her family had celebrated, Natalie missed it.

According to Nat's speculations, spring was near. Their altitude wouldn't allow for the greens of Iowa. Snow still covered the grounds. From the windows of the suite, no other homes could be seen. She literally believed at times she was confined to the snow globe of her first impression.

The suite she shared with Dexter had walls of shelves filled with books, the old kind with paper and spines. It was more than she'd had in what she referred to as *her room*. Though there was nothing to connect her to life beyond her snow globe, the books became her salvation. After breakfast, exercise, lunch, *Dexter-time*, and bath, which now often happened with Dexter in a spacious glass shower, Natalie had some time in the afternoon and evenings to herself. Those were the occasions where she'd disappear into the pages of fiction. It was a better alternative than remembering those she'd left behind.

With time, Nat was allowed to join Dexter in other areas of the house. If the staff were present, it was another reason to wear clothes. However, she was never alone. Those outings always included him. She still didn't know what he did for a living, but on the first floor, he had a large office with many computer screens. It was something about stocks, margins, options...she should have paid better attention to her classes at Harvard.

It was late one night as they lay together in bed that Dexter's words smashed Nat's snow globe, leaving glass shards to litter her world. "We've been gone for months. I need to be back in the United States."

Her heart raced as she lifted her panic-stricken eyes to his. "Are you going to leave me here alone?"

He pulled her warm, naked body closer until her head rested upon his shoulder. "No, bug. I'm never leaving you, and you're never leaving me, remember? But we'll need to fly."

She lifted her head again. "Please, Dexter. No cocktail."

His eyes closed as he exhaled. "I remember you saying you didn't want it. I'm conflicted. I have it ready for you. I don't know...you haven't shown me that you'll behave and not leave me, given the chance."

"I won't," she answered quickly.

"Oh, bug. I believe you mean that now, but it'll be different when given the opportunity. In the States, communication will be easy. You could even be recognized."

Recognized? Would she be? Now that she lived in a suite with mirrors, she wondered if she even looked the same as she had. Her reflection somehow seemed different. In so many ways, she wasn't the same girl who'd boarded the plane in Boston.

Besides, what did she want the world to know? What did they know about her disappearance? Would she want people to know who she'd become, that she enjoyed the way Dexter treated her...even when she didn't? That by making himself her entire world, he'd given her new purpose and a sense of being loved, not as a child or sibling, but as a woman?

Natalie shook her head. "Please, Dexter. I don't want to feel the way that cocktail made me feel. I don't like being out of control."

"You have no control."

It was a simple statement, yet accurate. She nodded. "You're right. However, I'd rather give it over to you willingly than unconsciously."

"I know. But you have to trust me."

"I do. I trust you. Please trust me. I remember that I'm your queen. What we do behind closed doors is our business, no one else's." Her heart ached, but the words were true. "I'd never want others to know that Natalie Rawlings kneels for hours or welcomes your punishment, that what you do to me makes me wet and wanting. That I crave the pain as much as the pleasure. It's true, you know it is. I'll continue to do it—for you and for me—but it's no one else's business."

"What about your family? What's their business?"

Natalie sat up, suddenly chilled as her old and new life collided.

Dexter followed her up and again wrapped her in his embrace. Tears she didn't expect cascaded down her cheeks.

"Shhh," he soothed. "Nat, it's something we both have to address if we're back in the States."

"What can I even say to them? I disappeared." She hiccupped. "I walked through customs with you of my own will. I left them." More tears. "How could they ever forgive me? I moved on without a word."

"You didn't."

Her expression questioned as her words followed suit. "What do you mean?"

"I told you to trust me. I wanted you. Now you're mine. I told you in the very beginning that I wasn't trying to remove you from your family or the other way around. We just needed time alone before we added them to the mix."

Natalie's skin prickled as myriad emotions flooded her system. "I don't understand."

Dexter eased from the bed. "Don't leave the bed, bug. I'll show you something that'll help this all make sense."

Nearly an hour later, Natalie looked up from Dexter's tablet, her eyes red and swollen. From what she'd read, he was right: she hadn't missed a thing. On every milestone, holiday, and birthday *Natalie* had communicated with her family. She'd sent pictures of landmarks with long-winded emails explaining her need to find herself after the debacle that was her college experience.

There were responses from both her father and mother. Though at first their words reflected their disappointment, with time, they both forgave, claiming they wanted nothing more than her return. Even her siblings corresponded. Not surprisingly, Nichol was more critical; however, like their parents, they both wanted her to come back.

When she turned toward him, Dexter asked, "Do you understand?"

Nat shook her head. Cognitively she understood everything she'd read. It was the reasoning behind it that she had a difficult time comprehending.

"You also sent text messages, mostly to your mother."

Her mother.

More tears.

"Why?" It was the only question she could form.

"For you. For them."

She scrolled the screen of his tablet. The emails dated back to a few days after her flight.

"Did they...did they look for me?"

"Of course they did." He kissed her forehead. "They love you. They love the selfish, spoiled daughter and sister they knew." His eyes shone like a clear ocean pool. "Wait until they see you now."

Natalie tried to process. She'd given up hope of ever seeing them again. She'd been so sure they'd save her, but when they didn't...

"You did this for me?"

"Yes."

As his answer rang in her ear, a wave of indignation washed over her. "The date. You started this right after you took me."

"Yes."

"All those questions you asked...the ones where you wanted truthful answers. You used what I told you to make these emails sound like they were coming from me." Each of her statements grew louder in volume, the words quick and staccato.

"Nat, watch your tone."

"My tone?" The emails brought back the woman she'd been. The two personas were at battle and the Natalie Rawlings of old was the one speaking. "My tone! You took me away from my family and made it sound like I was on vacation. This..." She shook the tablet in her grasp. "...wasn't for me or them. It was for you!"

Dexter's eyes darkened.

She didn't stop. "You did it so they wouldn't find me, so you could keep me, and..." She met his gaze. As their eyes connected, her chest grew heavy with the guilt of her words.

He had taken her. He had hurt her—that was what she'd been about to say. But he'd also freed her in a way she couldn't describe. He'd showed her a side of herself that she never knew, but now appreciated. He expanded her world by limiting it.

Natalie knew in her heart that she should apologize for raising her voice and accusing him. The narrowing of his eyes was telling her she should. But she couldn't. The conflict was back. Dexter's actions may have saved her relationship with her family, but they also stopped the worldwide search she'd at one time prayed for.

Her shoulders straightened as she braced for his retaliation.

What would be the price for her outburst?

"Are you done?"

Was she?

Nat lowered her eyes, still unable to vocalize an apology. Instead, she took on the appropriate posture. "Yes."

Dexter lifted her chin. "You're right," he said calmly. "It was for me, to give us time. It was also for you." When she didn't respond, he released his hold, stood, and pointed to the floor. "Nat."

Setting the tablet on the bed, her heart rate accelerated. She deserved his punishment. And despite the fact they'd made love only an hour ago, the anticipation of what he would do dampened her core as she slid to the floor and knelt at Dexter's feet.

"Tell me what should happen, what your outburst should cost."

Her pussy clenched and breasts throbbed. This shouldn't bring her body to life. His threatening tone shouldn't make her as excited as she was frightened, but it did.

Natalie leaned forward until her face was near the floor and kissed the tops of his feet. With each inch she lowered, her anger melted away. When she sat back up, supporting herself on her bent toes, she replied, "I'll take your punishment, my king. I was wrong. I should thank you for what you did. I guess it scares me. It's my two lives coming together. I never thought they would. I want to see my parents. I miss them, but I don't want to lose you."

He reached for her shoulders and lifted her to standing. "You won't lose me. I won't lose you." He lifted her chin again. "As I said, your family will see you for the queen you've become, not the spoiled princess you once were. While you were away from them, you received a tremendous gift. You went without to learn to appreciate."

His gift settled deep into her heart. She recalled the room in the basement, the cold, damp air, the musty water from the old pipes. The bed where they'd just been settled, covered in colorful comforters, was heaven compared to where she'd awoken.

Her eyes met his. "You're right. I do. I see things differently now. Thank you, Dexter, for showing me."

He kissed her softly. "You're welcome. Now, turn around, bug. Hands on the bed, feet apart. My belt will remind you who you're talking to and that outbursts and disrespectful tones are unacceptable."

Her pussy throbbed as she obeyed. Biting her lip to keep her smile at bay, she turned her face back over her shoulder until their gazes met. With veiled eyes, she asked, "Not your hand?"

Dexter grinned as he ran his hand over her ass, dipping his fingers between her wet folds.

She squirmed at his touch.

"No, my queen. I'd say that you like my hand on your ass too much. This needs to teach you a lesson."

CHAPTER 21

The best solutions are often simple,
yet unexpected. ~ Julian Casablancas

Natalie paced nervously about their suite. Her hands were clammy and posture straight. She was hot and then she was cold. It would be easy to say she was ill, but that wasn't it. Her attention went to the large windows. Snow still covered the ground and trees. Inside, it was warm—too warm. She tugged at her sweater. Circling the collection of suitcases, she shook her head. There were so many. It was everything they possessed in the villa. It seemed ridiculous. She'd never worn half of the clothes, and now they were taking them back to the States. There was also makeup and jewelry, accessories she'd only seen until today.

Today she was dressed and made up. She was prepared to leave.

And she wasn't.

The clothes covering her body were worse than Dexter's restraints. Somehow she'd grown accustomed to being without. The black turtleneck sweater itched, its soft yarn threatening to suffocate her. Natalie tugged again at the material around her throat.

It wouldn't choke her. She knew that. However, the restrictiveness was testing her nerves. The gray wool slacks flowed over the heeled boots and were bound too tightly at her waist. It wasn't that she was heavy or that the slacks fit improperly; it was that she hadn't worn pants of any kind in months. Even in the sitting room or around the villa, when she was clothed, she wore dresses. The heels were another issue. Though she'd walked in high heels from a young age, it had taken her a few days to do so again without resembling a gorilla playing dress up. Even the designer brands pinched her toes. The bra and panties were the absolute worst. Why did people wear them?

Her heart beat faster as she wrung her hands. Maybe it wasn't the clothes. It was everything. It was too much. They were leaving their haven. And the world beyond these walls scared her. She could please Dexter within these walls; would she be able to outside of them?

Natalie was also concerned about their flight. She'd never do or say anything to upset Dexter, much less incriminate him. Not because she feared his punishment, but because she loved him. Yet she couldn't stop thinking about the cocktail. Dexter hadn't said if she would drink it or not. They'd discussed it many times, each time with her promising to behave.

She replayed their conversations and his concerns. Though she hadn't had an opportunity to prove to him that she would behave in public, it seemed as though she'd proven she would behave. The only reason it hadn't been in public was that they'd yet to leave the villa. As she stared out the window, she imagined returning to the States and regaining the ability to communicate. If she dug deep enough, there was a small part of her—a very small part—that wanted to rebel. He was right: she couldn't do it in Austria, but she could in the States.

Could Dexter sense that small part?

Of course, he could. He saw Natalie like no one else could. He knew her thoughts and feelings before she did. Would he punish her for those ideas, or worse, make her drink his behavior-altering concoction?

As she tried to push her worries out of mind, her reflection caught her attention. She paused. It was her, yet it wasn't. Not only was she fully clothed, but even her hair was styled, in a low bun. She lifted her chin and stared into her own green eyes. Had she changed as Dexter said?

Quite possibly.

There was something regal in her stance. Was it something she'd always had or was it because now she was Dexter's queen? She was proud to be on his arm, beside him, and in his bed.

She spun as the bedroom door opened.

Dexter stood motionless, his hand on the large knob as he took her in. As it had many months ago, his gaze burned, leaving a trail of charred remains over her skin. This time it wasn't because she was naked, but because she wasn't.

As time ticked away and he didn't speak, she finally did. "I-it's what you told me to wear, what was laid out."

Without a word, Dexter took a step toward her and then another, until he was right before her. His eyes never left her, their blues and greens swirling like a turbulent sea. Finally, he looked down to the necklace's pendant lying upon her breasts and picked it up. Within his grasp he ran the large swirled silver charm through his fingers, and then let it fall back to her chest.

Her breath stilled, unsure of his thoughts.

"You're stunning."

Nat sighed. "I-I feel so...claustrophobic."

"I have something that may help. A solution I think will work."

"No," she replied quickly, her eyes filling with tears. "Please. Please trust me. Please don't make me drink it." She would if he insisted. He wouldn't need to trick her this time. She'd do it simply because he told her to, but she didn't want to.

Dexter's expression morphed from confusion to a grin. "No, bug. That's not what I'm talking about."

She let out a long breath, her chest falling accentuated by the tight black ribbed sweater.

He took her hand, stepped back, and encouraged her to spin. Like the small dancer inside her childhood jewelry box, she pirouetted. His gaze lightened as he admired her curves from every angle. "Simply stunning."

When their eyes met again, she responded, "Should I be concerned that you seem to find me more attractive with clothes on than without?"

"That isn't true. You're always ravishing. It's that I'm not used to seeing you like this. In this..." He motioned up and down. "...you resemble the girl I watched from afar, but the difference is that I now know what's under those clothes. Perhaps there's something enticing in having it all hidden, in knowing that I'm the only one who knows what's beneath the wrapping." He traced a rib of the sweater from below her neck to her breast. "I'm the only who knows how incredible your breasts look engorged and needy with your nipples clamped."

Nat's eyes fluttered as her insides tightened.

His hand moved to her behind. "How your radiant skin glows when it's marked by my hand or a crop." He slowly brought his hand upward, feathering her hips, ribs, and moving along the swell of her breast. It was as if he were worshiping what he couldn't see, making love to her with only words. When he reached her chin, he grasped it gently, causing her eyes to open. "To know how your gorgeous eyes sparkle with joy during both pleasure and pain." He softly kissed her cheek. "And how you give me the great honor of sharing both your smiles and your tears."

"Dex-ter..." She elongated his name as her nipples hardened under the bra and sweater.

"My Nat, you take my breath away every time I see you. Every time my eyes land upon you, from the first time until forever. I'm lost to you. I've told you that you don't have control, but that's not true. You hold the real power. Only you could break my heart."

She shook her head. "Never."

"Whether dressed for a plane ride, a gala, or naked and broken, never doubt that I see you as anything other than ravishing and alluring because under all the wrapping, you're lovely, inside and out."

Her cheeks warmed as she melted toward him, her breasts flattening against his hard chest. "I just want to make you happy."

"You do, simply by being you. You don't have to try."

She took a step back and looked down at the clothes she detested a few minutes ago. Maybe they weren't so bad. Shrugging, she asked, "So this is all right? You're okay with me wearing this?"

Dexter laughed as he once again scanned her up and down. "Today. Yes. I don't think escorting you naked onto our plane would be appropriate. I believe people may talk." He lifted his brow. "But once we're in the air...?"

"Our plane?" she asked.

"I don't fly commercially...unless there's a reason. I know you chose it willingly last time you flew. How did that work out for you?"

It was Nat's turn to laugh. "At first, not so great. But now, I'm content."

"Content?"

"More than content, Dexter. I have everything because I have you."

He winked. "I think from now on we'll stick with private."

"Okay. Does that mean I don't need to—?"

Dexter touched his finger to her lips, stopping her request. He then tugged her hand leading her to the sofa near the large bedroom windows.

Following his lead, she sat, their knees touching.

"I told you I had something that may help you feel better. I didn't mean the cocktail."

"What...?"

He slid from the sofa to one knee.

The small hairs on the back of her neck stood to attention. Their positioning was wrong. She belonged on the floor.

"Natalie Rawlings..." He reached into his pocket and pulled out a ring, a diamond ring. The most beautiful ring Natalie had ever seen.

"The last time we flew, I told you that one day you'd earn real rings. I also promised you that they were more exquisite than the fake ones. I hope you agree. They've been in my family for a few generations. What I didn't know when I told you that was that you are more exquisite than I ever imagined. You are my love, my life, and my queen. I've promised to never leave you nor to ever let you go, but before we board our plane, I hope that we can make it official.

"Natalie, will you be my wife? Will you fulfill your promise to never leave me, to always love me, and to be all that I need?"

Before she could answer, he added, "And I will do everything in my power to be all that you need."

As he spoke, Natalie lost focus of the ring. All that she saw was the loving admiration from the man she worshipped, adored, and loved. He was the man who had seen her at her lowest and lifted her to heights she never previously knew existed. He was her devil and her king. She was his, body and soul. She ran her fingers through his blond hair. "Dexter, I love you."

"Bug, I love you too. That isn't an answer."

She nodded. "It is. It's the answer to every question you ask me for the rest of our lives. I love you. I trust you. I'm yours. I'll be your wife and your queen, or your companion and your slave. I'll be whatever you want me to be."

He lifted her left hand and slipped the stunning diamond onto her fourth finger. "My wife and my queen, forever."

Natalie nodded. "Yes, I'll marry you." And then she, too, slipped from the sofa to her knees. "And I'll always bow to you."

Their lips came together as they sealed the deal.

"Marry now?" she asked, not sure how she felt about it. Nevertheless, if it was what he wanted, she wouldn't hesitate.

"Wouldn't you rather plan it with your mother?"

The fear from before returned as her chin fell forward.

He lifted her face. "Bug?"

"Yes," she said, "I do want that. I left them. I don't want to take my wedding away from them too."

He smiled. "Then we won't. We'll wait."

"But what if they don't want me back?"

"I showed you the emails. Nat, they want you back."

She took a deep breath. "I don't think I can face them without you."

"I'll be right there."

Later, as Dexter helped Natalie with her wool coat, she thought once again about how heavy the material was on her shoulders. And then as the large front door to the villa opened to the waiting car, the fresh mountain spring air made her appreciate the covering. It also took her breath away. The bright sun upon the snow was blinding as the wind nipped her cheeks.

Had it not been for Dexter's strong hand in the small of her back, she wasn't sure she'd have been able to step out into the world. It was too much sensation...too much everything.

"Are you all right?" he asked, once they were settled in the backseat of the sedan.

Natalie nodded. "I am because you're here." Her green eyes opened wider. "Dexter, what's my name?"

He tilted his head. "Your name?"

"My passport?"

Dexter reached for a small handbag that he must have put into the car earlier. Opening the clutch, he removed a slender wallet. "Here."

Her hands trembled as she opened the clasp. In the transparent compartment was her driver's license—her real one. She tugged out the credit cards, reading the name. They weren't the ones she had before, yet each one said the same name: Natalie Rawlings.

ALEATHA ROMIG

Her eyes filled with tears as she reached for the clutch and looked inside. Nestled within a narrow pocket was her passport, the one she'd used to board the plane over four months ago in Boston. Finally, she looked back to the man she loved. "My old credit cards...these are new?"

"You're mine. It's my responsibility to take care of your needs. Your old cards were from your parents. Their job is done."

"Thank you."

"Is that what you want, for your name on the cards and IDs to be that?"

Natalie shook her head. "Not forever. Now, I do. But eventually, I'd like it to read Smithers."

Dexter took the wallet and passport and put them back into the bag. Handing her the purse, he said, "One day, my queen."

CHAPTER 22

Peace cannot be kept by force;
it can only be achieved by understanding. ~ Albert Einstein

"They just took off? From where? Where are they landing?" Tony asked, his dark eyes focused on the man sitting on the other side of the desk.

"Please say the United States," Claire said, her emerald green eyes also on the man with the information.

It didn't matter that it was before sunrise or that Tony Rawlings and his wife had been asleep only thirty minutes ago. It didn't matter that they were sitting in their home office in Iowa with bathrobes over their sleeping clothes.

There was very little the three people in the room didn't know about one another.

They'd been a family in most senses of the word. They may not have the same last name or the same blood running through their veins, but Phil Roach knew long ago that there was nothing he wouldn't do to protect the woman in this room. He loved his wife, body and soul. He also loved Claire Rawlings. Her heart had been stolen before he met her. That didn't mean he wouldn't be all he could be for her. She was the sister he never had.

Phil had failed her in the past. He'd also killed for her and would again. And with Claire came her husband and their children. Phil had been there the horrible night Nichol came into the world. Of all the things Phil Roach had done, all the things he'd seen...that night was one of the worst of his memories.

That didn't mean he didn't love Nichol like a niece. That he didn't love them all, Nate and Natalie too. He did. He was their uncle, the one who protected and watched over them. That was why these past four months had been so difficult. Natalie wasn't simply his employers' daughter. She was his family, too.

"According to the manifest filed in Graz, Austria," Phil said, "the chartered Gulfstream G650 will eventually land in Burlington, Vermont."

Tony shook his head. "There's too much in that fucking sentence. How in the hell did they stay under the radar for this long?"

Phil looked at Tony and then Claire. "Graz, Austria, still doesn't tell us exactly where they were. The countryside is too open. What matters now is that they're coming back. The manifest confirms the names. Natalie is flying under her real name."

"She hasn't said she's coming home in the text messages or emails," Claire said, her hands wrapped around a warm cup of coffee. She wasn't planning on getting any more sleep, not that she'd had much in the last four months.

"That's because they don't want a welcoming party at the airport," Tony said, "but that's exactly what they're going to get."

Claire and Phil both looked back to Tony, silently questioning his statement.

"What?" he asked.

Leaving her coffee behind, Claire stood and walked a small circle. This was the same office Tony had designed for the two of them years ago—a dual office, with desks for both of them. It was their shared space, nothing like his home office when she'd first met her husband. "I'm not sure that's a good idea," she finally said.

"Why the fuck not? Our daughter's been missing for four months."

"She's been communicating," Phil said.

"It wasn't her. It was Diane Yates."

"The text messages were from Diane," Phil confirmed. "But not the emails. Taylor is on her way to Vermont. She'll get visual confirmation of the passengers as soon as the plane lands. I'm just concerned..." His voice trailed away as he shared a glance with Claire.

"Tony," Claire interjected, "we can't push her away."

Her husband stood. "Push her away? Of course not. I'm going to push that damn Smithers man away. Smithers..." His head shook.

Once they had the name and confirmed Jonas Dexter Smithers's identity, it didn't take long to put the pieces they had gathered together. Yet the picture was still incomplete. There were more pieces to assemble.

"It won't work. You can't," Claire reasoned.

"I damn well can," his voice boomed. "I can bring our daughter home and ground her to this house if I have to."

She shook her head. "No, you can't."

"She's an adult," Phil volunteered.

"Well, she sure as hell hasn't acted like one."

Claire sighed as she sat back down, her small frame landing in the plush white leather desk chair. "I'd bet all of our fortune on the fact that she has."

"Running away to *find herself*...hiding in the middle of the Alps. That's not acting like an adult."

"Tony," Claire tried to reason, "if the emails are true—even if they weren't written by her—if they're true, she's in love with this man."

"She's not in love. She's lost."

"That isn't your decision to make. She's been with him now for a while. I would say our little girl has been doing adult things."

Tony shook his head. "I'll kill him."

"Phil," she said, ignoring Tony's threat, "please ask Taylor to take pictures of the passengers. I want to see my daughter."

"When are they landing?" Tony asked.

Phil looked down at the tablet in his hand. "The plane just left Graz. A Gulfstream G650 can make good time, and it won't need to stop for fuel on the way. They should land in Burlington in..." He looked at his watch. "...close to twelve hours. That should get them to their destination by near 5:00 PM our time, 6:00 PM in Vermont."

"That's plenty of time," Tony said. "Claire and I will be dressed and ready to fly in an hour. I'll call for the plane."

Claire shook her head. "Please listen. I hope I'm wrong, but all I can base my feelings on is that I'm her mother—"

"And I'm her father."

"I know what it's like to be in love with someone whom your family doesn't like."

Tony's brown eyes darkened. "This isn't the same."

"Of course not, but no matter how they met—on the plane, during her travels...whatever—the fact remains that if she's in love with him, her father stealing in and whisking her home won't stop her feelings. It won't stop his."

"If he's dead, it will."

"Tony."

Her husband took a deep breath and sat, leaning back.

Claire continued, "What are we going to do, lock her in her room?"

His eyes shut.

"I'm serious. I love Natalie. I will not lose my daughter again. If she's back in the States and we can be sure where she is and that she's safe, we need to wait."

"I've never been a patient man," Tony said.

Claire's gaze swept to Phil, seeing the same grin on him as she had growing over her own lips. They both knew Tony's statement to be true. He was a lot of things but patient wasn't one of them. "Let's be sure it's really her. Let's be sure she's at least back in the country."

"I know it isn't Diane," Phil said. "Taylor called her as soon as we got the report. Diane was told to mail all Natalie's documents to an address in Germany. We tracked the address when she told us. It was an attorney's office. No one there claims to have a client by the name of Smithers. No one remembers receiving a package and then resending it. Despite the tracking numbers, they all seem to have a severe case of amnesia."

"Why didn't I know about that?" Claire asked as Tony sat forward.

"It didn't mean anything. We were waiting to learn more," Phil said.

"What else haven't you told us?" Tony asked.

"Jonas Smithers doesn't use his first name. He uses his second, Dexter. That's why the name wasn't matching with the name mentioned in her emails. The emails were correct—Dexter. He's a weather-derivatives trader by profession. He also inherited his parents' fortune when they died. His father, as you know, was very successful in real estate."

Tony shook his head. "I didn't know. I lost track of him. I've been a little wrapped up in all things Rawlings."

"The Rawlings Corporation offices in Boulder, Colorado, are housed in a building owned by JS Enterprises."

"JS is Jonas?"

"Was," Phil said. "He died two years ago. His wife, second wife, was killed in an automobile accident a few months later. The son seems to be doing very well managing his parents' portfolio. He doesn't do it alone; he has a team. But it's the weather-derivatives where he's making a name for himself."

"Weather-derivatives?" Claire asked. "I studied meteorology, and I don't know what that is."

"I admit I had to do some research," Phil said. "Basically, weather is a tradable commodity."

"How do you trade weather?"

Phil shook his head. "It has to do with qualifying weather in terms of averages, attaching a dollar amount, and packaging it."

"I don't understand," Claire said.

"It doesn't fucking matter," Tony added. "The point is that Jonas's son is wealthy. We can't buy our daughter back with money."

"Our daughter isn't a tradable commodity!"

"I didn't say she was. I was just speaking from experience. Everything has a price."

Claire looked at her husband. "Nat didn't have one. Nat wasn't in debt or tending bar."

"That's not what I meant," Tony said. "I mean that everyone and everything has a price. Take that painting hanging in the sitting room."

"The Salvador Dali piece?"

Tony nodded. "What would you be willing to sell it for?"

Claire shook her head. "Nothing. You bought it for me while we were on our anniversary trip. It's priceless."

"So the price isn't monetary. If I offered you Natalie back home with you for that painting, would you trade it?"

"In a heartbeat," she said.

"See. You have a price." Tony looked to Phil. "So money isn't Smithers's price; we need to find out what is. If you two are so sure that we shouldn't bring her back home by force, we'll figure out another way to get her home."

"Maybe we won't."

Tony looked to Claire. "What are you saying?"

"I'm saying that Natalie is growing up—she's grown up. So are our other children. Nate's been living in London for the last year. Nichol is in New York. Natalie isn't going to live here forever."

"She's not staying with him."

"I want our children to be happy. Don't you?"

"Of course," he said.

"Maybe she's happy with him. She obviously wasn't happy at Harvard. We just need to understand."

Tony shook his head. "We need to know what the hell happened. *I* need to see her."

Phil nodded. "What about meeting the plane? I still think it's best to let Taylor get the visual. If Natalie appears well, then perhaps not make contact."

"I agree," Claire said, "but if Taylor has any reason to worry—"

"If she does, she's prepared to step in."

Tony leaned back. "Where are they going in Vermont? What about his address? Surely he isn't planning on disappearing into the mountains again."

"Not technically. We have his address. He lives in the foothills of Mount Mansfield. The estate is large."

Claire sighed. "Please let us know that she's safe, first. I want to talk to her. I want to hold her and hug her."

"We're a step closer," Phil said.

Claire looked at the clock in the corner of her computer screen. "Only eleven more hours."

"It's going to be a long day," Tony agreed. "I say we have more coffee."

Their gaze met as she grinned. "Do you want me to get it?"

"No," he said with a shake of his head. "I wouldn't want to put you out."

CHAPTER 23

There are times when fear is good. It must keep its watchful place at the heart's
controls. There is wisdom won from pain. ~ Aeschylus

To her relief, Natalie avoided Dexter's cocktail on their flight. She would have behaved around the airport and airplane people even without the engagement ring. However, every time she looked down and saw the glistening stone—a family heirloom—she was reminded of the man she loved.

The man who made her heart beat faster.

The man she trusted with her life and her future.

While the plane descended through the pre-dusk sky, Natalie watched her new home state come into view through the small window. They weren't landing at their house, but in a neighboring city. From the air, it didn't look large. What she noticed the most was the color.

Had color always meant as much to her as it did now?

Nat wasn't sure. She just knew that after living in black and white for months, colors were more vibrant than they'd ever been. It was another gift she'd received, learning to appreciate the things that never before seemed important.

"Tell me your thoughts," Dexter said, squeezing her hand.

"It's so green."

He smiled as he leaned closer, peering past her to the window. "Yes. After being in the snow for so long, I suppose it is."

Natalie started to say that she hadn't been in the snow. She'd been inside. Leaving the villa for the plane was the first time she'd been outdoors in nearly four months. Her inside detention had been acceptable while she imagined herself within a snow globe. After all, there was nowhere to go in a snow globe. But now, she was seeing the world again. Even though the sun was setting, it would be there. Places to go. Things to see.

"Bug?"

"Yes?" she asked, her voice far away, like her thoughts.

"You're overthinking; I can feel it. Talk to me."

"When we get to your house—"

"Our home," he interrupted.

She nodded. "When we get to *our home*, will you...will it...?" She wasn't sure how to verbalize her question. It seemed immature to ask about something as simple as being allowed to go outdoors, and yet, that was now her life, the one she chose when she accepted Dexter as her king.

The plane touched down with barely a bounce.

"We'll be in the car soon. What are you trying to ask?"

"It was okay to stay in the villa all day and night, because the outside was nothing but cold, but now..." She watched his eyes, wondering if he understood.

"Are you asking if you'll be allowed to leave our home?"

Her pulse quickened at the verbalization. It sounded different in her thoughts. As she struggled with the tug between her heart and mind, she hoped that somehow she could help Dexter understand her dilemma. "I don't want to *leave*. I just don't want to be kept inside. It's spring. The weather is warming..." She allowed her words to trail away, afraid if she presented too much of a case, it would be too hard on her heart if he said no.

Dexter hummed his understanding. "What do you think?"

Her insides pinched as she gave into her heart. "I think it's up to you."

"And?"

"And I trust you to make the right decision."

He leaned over and kissed her cheek. Reaching for her seatbelt, he unsnapped it. "Let's go. I know you've been raised with wealth, but I'm excited for you to see our home. I don't think you'll be disappointed."

Sensing his excitement, Natalie smiled. Her request would wait.

As the attendant opened the door, stairs descended.

In simply the amount of time it took the plane to land, the sky darkened to velvet black. Maybe it wasn't totally dark; it was that they were surrounded by lights. The tarmac was a rush of activity. So many people. Nat reached for Dexter's hand as she fought to breathe.

Too many people. What could she say or do?

People had never bothered her before, but now they overwhelmed her. Everything within her wanted to hide in Dexter's arms or maybe run back to the plane. However, she was now his queen. A queen didn't run away. With her chin held high she looked over her new kingdom.

As she and Dexter politely said goodbye to the pilot and attendants, they walked down the stairs, hand in hand. The Vermont air was fresh and cool—not as cold as Austria. It was springtime and she was back where there would be beautiful flowers and budding trees. Her mother had taught her an appreciation of nature.

A golf cart type of vehicle waited near the plane to take Natalie and Dexter to a garage where their car was also waiting. As they settled on the seat, she again wished for the security of walls. Being exposed, to the night as well as curious eyes, was overwhelming. Everything was too much.

Within a few minutes, they entered the hangars and garages. Again, there were so many workers. Instead of concentrating on her trepidation, she recalled Dexter's words —what he'd said when he first told her they'd be coming back to the States.

He'd been right: Natalie could run here. Not with him beside her, but she could. She could tell someone what had really happened—what went on behind closed doors. She could speak the language and communicate. The thought was like the blowing breeze, there and then gone.

Just because Natalie could run didn't mean she wanted to. The blue-green eyes looking down lovingly at her, the way his leg touched hers, and the warmth of his hand over her thigh all confirmed what her heart knew: she wouldn't tell anyone. She wouldn't try to leave the man who owned her heart, body, and soul.

Dexter lifted her left hand and kissed her knuckles, beside the large shining diamond. "You've done very well, my bug."

The moniker no longer bothered her. Instead, her blood warmed at his tone, radiating in a pink glow from her now-blushed cheeks. Before she could reply, the cart came to a stop.

A tall gentleman wearing a driver's uniform and standing near the open door to a large black SUV spoke, "Mr. Smithers, welcome home."

"Thank you, Jinx." He motioned to Natalie. "Let me introduce my fiancée, Miss Rawlings."

Natalie momentarily looked up to Dexter. He'd said her name as if it weren't a name that could be recognized. And then she remembered her manners and moved her gaze to Jinx. "Hello." She extended her hand.

"It's a pleasure to meet you, Miss Rawlings."

Nat considered correcting Jinx and telling him to call her Natalie—most of the Rawlings staff always had—but then Miss Rawlings was the name Dexter used. If she corrected Jinx, she'd be correcting Dexter.

"And you, also," she simply replied.

Out of the corner of her eye, she saw a flash, or was it her imagination? Had someone taken their picture? Was this what it would be like to be back in the States? Had she been a missing person? Were people looking for her?

She instinctively turned her head away from the flash and toward Dexter.

Nat knew from experience what it was like to be sought after by paparazzi. It wasn't unusual for the Rawlings family to become faux news, as if their outings were newsworthy events. That was the reason they traveled to the island. The seclusion and anonymity was refreshing.

"What is it?" Dexter asked.

Nat wasn't sure. "I don't know. I think I'm just exhausted."

Releasing her hand, he wrapped his arm around her shoulder and pulled her closer. "Let's go home."

"Yes." Her green eyes lit up. "Home. I like the sound of that."

Dexter kissed her forehead as they got into the SUV.

There were other members of the staff to whom Natalie was introduced. She was the queen and always addressed as Miss Rawlings.

With each passing day, Nat adjusted to their change of scenery and to the estate in Vermont. Like Dexter's home in Austria, this estate was secluded and luxurious. Her behavior on the flight and in public was rewarded with forward momentum in her liberties and freedoms.

It could have been different.

After about a week in Vermont, Dexter took Natalie's hand and led her downstairs. "I want to show you something."

At first she was excited. There were so many beautiful aspects of his home. When they'd first entered the lowest level, they'd found a beautifully furnished basement with a large room for entertaining, a theater room, and a gym complete with the best exercise equipment. However, as they went lower and farther into the depths of the basement, she had an overwhelming sense of déjà vu.

It was as he directed her to a room he'd left out of their first tour that her skin covered in perspiration and her stomach knotted. It was a room he'd had constructed especially for her. Like the place she'd awakened months ago, this room was hidden, its entrance camouflaged.

When her steps stuttered, he tugged her hand. "Don't stop. I had this made for you. It's another gift."

Tears filled her eyes. "Why? Please..."

He leaned down and kissed her cheek, tasting her tears. "I

wanted you to know that this is here. It's here to remind you of my rules. It's here if you need time to yourself to reflect or if I decide it's where you should be."

With her heart beating at triple time, she continued down the gray hallway and to the white wood door. It was an exact replica, all the way down to the musty air. She clung tightly to his hand. However, it was as the beep filled her ears and the large handleless door opened that she felt faint. He opened the inside door: white cement-block walls and a concrete floor. She looked up, but there was no window. "Dexter, I won't disappoint you. I want to please you, but I can do that better with you. Please don't make me go in there."

"You're not going alone. I'm with you."

It had been over a month since she'd been locked in her room in Austria. Taking the few steps through the doorway was more difficult than their first trip through customs. This time she knew what could be awaiting her.

"Please..." Her pleas went unheard, or perhaps they were only in her mind, because as she looked up at the stark white cinder-block walls, the door shut and they were both inside.

Somehow over the last month, she'd found Dexter's domination fun. It was. But as she slowly moved her gaze to the man before her, she didn't see the one who knelt on one knee and proposed or the one with the sparkling gaze who was excited to show her new things. She was, instead, transported back to the one who hurt her, demeaned her, the one who left her for hours on her knees or worse, on her toes and hanging by her wrists.

"Dexter." She stiffened her neck. "I know it's here. May we please go back upstairs?"

Instead of acknowledging her speech, his eyes darkened as he commanded, "Take off your clothes."

While the memories of her time in a similar room flooded her mind, she did as he bid.

She couldn't not.

It was her job to do as her king said. First, she stepped out of her shoes. The cold concrete floor added to her chill.

There was staff around the house that required her clothing. However, alone in this room, they weren't around the staff.

Next, Nat reached for the hem of her blouse and pulled it over her head. The friction of the material loosened her hair from its styled position. Her slacks were the next to go, down her legs. With the removal of each article of clothing, the cool air prickled her flesh, eliciting goose bumps until they piled one on top of the other and small hairs stood to attention. Dexter didn't speak, yet his watchful eyes never left her body, a hauntingly familiar gleam reflecting the steady flash of the camera in the corner. He hadn't tried to camouflage it.

Maybe that was worse?

Finally, with trembling fingers Natalie unlatched her bra and pulled down her panties.

Dexter didn't command her with words, nevertheless, she assumed the position, moving her legs to shoulder distance apart, turning her palms outward, and raising her chin. His murmur of appreciation was the only sound besides the tap of his boots as he walked, one, two, and three circles around her.

"Do you need a day or two in here to help you remember?"

Her mind screamed for her to say no, to beg for his understanding. Yet her heart dictated her response. "If it's your desire."

After all, he hadn't asked if she *wanted* to stay in the cell he'd had built. The answer to that question would be a resounding no. Dexter asked Nat if she *needed*...he was the one who determined her need. Nat's core clenched as fear combined with awe at her fiancé's power to control her entire life awakened her desire.

"Kneel."

Without hesitation, Nat fell to her knees, her bent toes supporting her weight as she kept her hands palms up.

"Are you wet, my queen?"

She shouldn't be. This was beyond their normal *Dexter-time.* This was the knowledge that he had planned for her misbehavior. Nonetheless she was. "Yes, my king."

Dexter gathered her hair, removing the loose pins, and then divided her locks in thirds. Next, he tenderly braided the length. As his fingers plaited the strands, tears fell from her eyes. He hadn't braided her hair since she was in the same kind of room back in the villa. He then re-secured the end with a ponytail tie from his pocket. "You're beautiful on your knees."

His words returned a small degree of the warmth the room had stolen.

Reaching for her chin, Dexter tipped her face upward until their gazes locked. "If you'd have misbehaved on our trip, I had this waiting."

She didn't speak.

"Now it's here if we need it. Will we need it?"

Again, *need.* "That's your decision."

Still holding her chin, he orchestrated her movements. "You're being a good girl. Will you do as I say?"

"Always."

"Take me out."

With her chin still held within his grasp, she couldn't see what her hands were doing, yet she obeyed. With nimble fingers, she quickly reached for his waist, unbuckled his belt, unfastened the button, and lowered the zipper.

"Remove my belt."

Her breathing slowed as she pulled the leather from the loops, her mind reeling with the possibility of his plans. Would he strike her? Would he restrain her? Her heart beat faster with each option.

"I'm going to fuck your mouth."

Her tongue darted to her lips as her nipples painfully hardened.

"Hands behind your back. You're going to take all of me."

Her pussy flooded as he looped his belt behind her neck. Accepting his control, she leaned back into the leather, opened her lips, and lowered her tongue to the floor of her mouth. He held each end of the belt, creating a support for her neck as he unceremoniously thrust his hard cock past her lips and deep into her throat. Musk filled her senses as he continued to press forward while pulling her toward him.

She couldn't breathe.

Tears overspilled her lids and cascaded down her cheeks as he pushed her limits. In and out. Stars burst behind her now-closed lids as her cells screamed for oxygen. Though her body wanted to fight, her mind slipped away as she floated in the sound of his voice. He praised her as he thrust, his voice deep and satisfied, his growls and groans keeping time to his rhythm. She was giving him pleasure—or he was taking it. The end result was the same. If the price was her pain or her life, she'd pay it.

And then he released her as she gasped for air.

"On the bed, bug."

It took her brain a moment to process. The black and white room was out of focus as dark ovals floated in her vision. On shaky legs, Nat stood. Dexter's strong grasp stopped her from falling as she worked to obey. The bed was bare, the mattress scratchy. Dexter rolled her to her stomach and pulled her arms together behind her back. She didn't complain as he secured them with the belt. Not because it didn't hurt, but her brain was still battling its short round of suffocation. She wasn't operating on all cylinders. Around and around, he wound the leather until her shoulders ached and she was bound from her elbows to her wrists.

He flipped her over and pushed her back, the rough surface abrading her skin. Teasing her breasts, he said, "I wish I had brought clamps."

She didn't speak until he bit hard on one nipple. And then it wasn't a word but a shriek.

He kissed her cheek. "That's it. Let me taste your tears and hear your cries. It makes me hard."

He dipped his head down and bit the other breast before sitting up and admiring his work. "My teeth marks are stunning on you."

"Dexter..." Her mind wasn't working to form complete sentences.

She soon forgot the discomfort as Dexter methodically descended on her body, covering her in kisses and nips, sucking and licking until he parted her legs. His weight upon her body pushed her shoulders against the mattress as he buried himself inside her.

The pleasure was short-lived.

A man on the brink of madness, Dexter took what was his. There was no gentleness, no tenderness. Natalie couldn't keep up as he continued to use her. There was no place he didn't go. Nothing he didn't do.

She could protest or beg, but what good would it do?

She belonged to him.

Instead of fighting, Natalie gave Dexter what he wanted: her body, cries, and tears.

CHAPTER 24

*The thing you fear most has no power. Your fear of it is what has
the power.
Facing the truth really will set you free.* ~ Oprah Winfrey

W eeks went by and they fell into their new routine. The
room in the basement was never mentioned again. It
was there in the back of Natalie's mind and there in reality. Yet
it was as if it weren't.

When that night finally ended, Dexter cradled Natalie's
battered body in his arms and carried her up to their suite.
She couldn't have made the trip if she'd tried. He tenderly laid

her in the large tub. His voice soothed as he soaked her in warm, sweet-smelling water and sponged her aching skin. Though she fought to stay conscious, her last memory was of the man she loved, the one who took care of her. The next morning when she awoke in their large soft bed, it was as if it never happened. The incident was never mentioned. Though it was as if it had been a nightmare, the bruises told her otherwise.

The ones on her arms and elsewhere had now faded. Nevertheless, for a while, only long sleeves and slacks or long dresses were acceptable to be worn around others. Dexter didn't mind seeing his marks, but they weren't to be shared with others. They were an outward sign of their bond. While he didn't mention the basement—or the incident, he admired the way the markings looked as the colors changed.

The bruises on Nat's soul were another story. Their color may have faded, but they remained as a reminder of the man omnipresent within the man she loved. She would do anything to avoid another trip to the cell in the depths of their home.

Natalie wasn't sure if what she knew in her heart and mind about that night had actually been said aloud; however, at some point through the basement ordeal, Natalie understood what was happening. She couldn't say if Dexter told her or if she sensed it. There were too many spots or voids in her memory of that night.

What occurred in the new basement room, in her rationalization, was the union Dexter had planned for Austria, before learning that Natalie was a virgin. It was the culmination of his planning—his reward. She belonged to him, all of her. But like everything else, he knew what was best. The timing was better this way. Had Dexter done to her on their first night in Austria what he'd done that night, they wouldn't be here now. He would have broken her. By waiting and taking it slowly, she would survive.

Over the months, he'd prepared her to accept whatever he gave.

Now, she was his—whatever he needed.

Now, she'd learned her place.

Each day that bled into another week earned Natalie more freedoms. Without the basement as an option, their *Dexter-time* returned to something she not only anticipated but often enjoyed. He tested her limits, but always guaranteed her pleasure.

Though Natalie had yet to leave the property by herself, she did with Dexter. At every turn, she proved her ability to behave. The man beside her on those outings was suave and debonair. He opened doors and pulled out chairs. He complimented and praised her. He talked to her and asked her opinion.

He worshipped his queen.

Together they enjoyed cute little family restaurants and driving on winding roads through the mountains. Sometimes Jinx drove. Other times it was just the two of them.

On one warm spring day, they stopped at a spot in the foothills with an amazing view and picnicked. Dexter surprised her with a blanket, basket of food, and drinks. His smile lit her soul. With no one else around them for miles, the blanket wasn't used only for eating.

It was difficult sometimes for Natalie to rationalize that the handsome man with light hair blowing in the breeze and shining ocean-hued eyes who made jokes and smiled lovingly at her was the same man who hurt her without remorse. However, he was. And with the exception of one night, she welcomed both of his needs into her life.

Their home was indeed marvelous. And while it was similar

in luxury to the world where she was raised, this was different. She was now the queen. Dexter was her king. Her love. Her salvation. He was also her tormentor and devil. There was no one else she needed as he filled every role.

Besides their suite, Nat's favorite place in her new home was the gardens. It had been the first freedom she requested, to go there and help tend the flowers, plants, and grasses. Even though Dexter explained that the gardeners took care of everything, she persisted.

Spending cool mornings pruning flowers had become one of her favorite times of day.

It didn't take long before she gained the liberty of moving about the house and yards. The pool area was stunning with fountains and shaded tables and beds. Their home was older than the one where she was raised. Grand and stately.

Now that they were in the States their schedule also changed. When they'd been in Europe Dexter had the luxury of working in different time zones. The reality of living and working in the same time zone now caused them to delay *Dexter-time* until later. Natalie never realized how accustomed she'd become to their routine. Now, after a day of gardening, reading, and exercising, she'd bathe and prepare. The anticipation of him returning from his office off the estate was greater than it had been waiting for his return to her room.

It was as he'd open the door to their suite to find her standing as he'd instructed and his aqua-blue gaze twinkled that her insides clenched. While it was different to have him leave during the day and go to his office away from home, the separation gave him time to come up with new ideas and implements for their reunion. Natalie didn't mind. Sometimes when she knew they weren't leaving the estate, she'd even braid her own hair. It was her invitation to his more taxing desires.

When she would, she could also depend upon some sort of punishment for doing what Dexter called *topping from the bottom.*

The thought made her smile. After all, it was what she was after in the first place.

Dexter Smithers was her everything. She was his. It was the way they both wanted it to be.

The queen who bowed only to her king.

Besides the experience of the one night, the most difficult part of coming back to the States was what Dexter had said they'd need to address—Natalie's family.

The first encounter occurred before he showed her his gift in the basement. They'd only been in Vermont for two days when Dexter brought Natalie his laptop. She was in their suite reading when he placed it on the table beside her.

"It's time, bug."

She looked at the computer as if it were a snake, its tail rattling and its head raised ready to strike. He hadn't told her she couldn't use technology; however, it was never present. He had computers in his office, but other than his tablet, there wasn't anything readily available. "Time for what?"

"We've been here for nearly forty-eight hours. I suspect your family knows that you're back. You need to email them. Your mom or dad, it's up to you."

Nat's head moved from side to side as her skin prickled. "No." She wasn't looking at Dexter, but at the venomous computer. She couldn't imagine what she'd say to them.

"Excuse me?"

His stern tone pulled her attention up from the laptop and back to him. Without hesitation, she slid from the sofa to his feet. Sitting back on her bent toes, she lowered her head. "I'll take your punishment. Just please, no email."

Dexter reached for her shoulders and helped her stand. "I'm not going to punish you. However, this isn't optional. You will sit here and write an email."

"Then that's punishment," she said under her breath.

Dexter shook his head. "Is this how you were with them?"

Her green eyes sought his meaning.

"Oh, bug, don't give me that innocent stare. You're being a brat. Is this the spoiled princess I watched from afar?"

His words struck harder than his belt.

"I'm not..."

"Yes, you are. You're flat-out refusing, topping from the bottom to avoid the email, and then talking back. That's not the behavior of my queen. Is this the way the spoiled princess acted?"

Nat sighed. "I-I don't know. I just don't want to do it."

"Did they allow you to get away with it?"

"Please, Dexter. I don't want to write them."

"Did they? That was a question."

"I don't know. I guess they did. I'm not ready."

"You are. I want you to do it now."

She turned toward the table. Staring at the laptop, she said, "I don't know what to say."

Dexter nudged her toward the sofa. "Come here."

Slowly, she did. He turned on the screen. There, before her, was the string of emails she'd read back in Austria. On the top was a new one. It was from her mom and by its bold print was marked unread. Her eyes widened as she looked back to Dexter. "Have you read it?"

"It hasn't been opened." When she didn't move, he clicked the trackpad. The email opened:

Nat,

I haven't heard from you for a while. Your dad and I are concerned.

Natalie, we miss you. We love you. We are here for you.

Your brother will be home in a few weeks. He'll only be here for a long weekend, but Nichol is coming, too. I wish with all my heart you were with us. Our family isn't complete without you.

Please write or call.

Love,

Mom

NATALIE READ it again before turning to Dexter. "Please, I'll write the email, but please don't make me go. I can't...not all of them."

"I think she knows you're back in the States."

"How?"

"I would suppose it isn't difficult to have a watch set for your name."

"Then I should have used that other identification."

"No," Dexter said again. "What you should do—what you will do —is sit here until you've responded to your mother. You're not moving. I'm not moving. We'll sit here until tomorrow, but the longer this takes, the sorer your ass is going to be. I'm not a patient man."

Natalie huffed as she turned back to the computer. He was right. He wasn't patient.

"Bug?"

"Fine."

"Bug?" His head was shaking at her tone.

"Yes, Dexter. I'll reply."

She sat, her fingers perched over the keyboard. Writing a simple email response shouldn't be this difficult. When she was at Harvard, she'd write ten-page essays without blinking an eye. Expressing herself through words written on a page was never a problem.

Until now.

Dear Mom,

She backspaced and erased the comma.

Dear Mom and Dad,

Her hands dropped to her lap. "I know they've received the emails, but I didn't write them. Will you..?" She looked up through her lashes. "...please, Dexter? You can write the words." This used to work with others, with her dad or Phil; she would ask nicely and they'd acquiesce.

Dexter didn't. Instead, he said, "Talk to me. What are you afraid of?"

She let out a breath. "Of seeing how much I hurt them. Of disappointing you. Of saying something I shouldn't say."

His expression softened. "They love you. I love you. You read the emails. You know what they've been told. They haven't been told we're engaged. Don't you think your family would want to know that? Tell them you're back in the States and that you're getting adjusted to the time change and learning your way around a new town."

"That's all true."

She nodded. "Can I tell them where I am?"

He shrugged. "In general terms. You're staying here with me in Vermont."

She suddenly realized the extent of her father's resources. It wasn't like she didn't know, but she remembered. "They'll come here. They know your name. You—I mean me—in the emails, told them. My dad..."

Dexter nodded. "I'm sure he has the ability to find us. I'd be surprised if they haven't already. But tell your mom you're embarrassed about leaving, missing Christmas, and upsetting her. Tell her the truth. That you want to see them, but not yet. And you're not ready for the whole family. Tell her that you and I will go together to Iowa once we're settled. Use me as an excuse. Say that I can't leave again so soon with my work."

"Okay." She could do that. Her fingers perched again over the keys.

Each word was easier than the last. By the time she finished the things Dexter had told her to write, she thought of other things she wanted to share. "Can I tell her about your gardens? My mom loves plants as much as I do."

"Yes, bug. Add what you want. Just let me read it before you hit send."

Once she began, her fingers flew. She described the home she was now sharing with Dexter. She talked about spring and how much she loved the colors. By the time she finally signed her name, she'd shed more than a few tears, but her heart was full.

She turned the computer to Dexter with a smile. "Will you tell me when she responds?"

"Yes."

After reading, he tapped send.

"You didn't change anything?"

"Why would I? Was that all true, the part about the house and flowers?"

"Yes," she said, leaning back against the soft material. "It's a beautiful home."

"One day we'll invite them here."

Again, Natalie eased from the sofa to Dexter's feet. This time, instead of sitting as he had taught her, she wedged her way between his knees. It was the way he fed her on some days long ago, far away. Looking up, she smiled. "Thank you. I love you."

"Are you glad you did it?"

She nodded. "You were right. I'm excited that I did, and I can't wait to hear back."

"The next step will be calling."

The smile faded from her face, her green eyes losing their shine.

"You won't be alone. I'll be there."

"Thank you, Dexter."

He petted her hair, tucking a loose strand behind her ears. "I love you, too, my Nat."

She looked from his ocean-blue gaze to his waist and back up. Biting her lip, she said, "It's up to you, my king. I'm not trying to take control, but right now, I'd really like to show you how much I appreciate your knowing what's best for me. I'm glad I wrote them. I am. You were right. And I wouldn't have done it without your prompting. When you decide it's time to call them, I'll do it."

"How?"

Her cheeks rose. "Definitely my hands, my mouth, and if you desire...anywhere else."

"In position, bug."

She wiggled to her knees as he leaned back. "Take it out. Let's start with a kiss."

Nat licked her lips as she unbuckled his belt. Her fingers worked nimbly as she freed his cock. By the time it was out, he was rigid with the tip glistening. One more look to his eyes and she leaned forward, opening her lips just enough to run them down his length.

"Kiss first," he reminded her.

She puckered, kissing the tip.

"Now."

Her heart was full as their suite filled with his deep growl.

CHAPTER 25

The greatest gift that you can give to others is the gift of unconditional love and acceptance. ~ Brian Tracy

Natalie's heart raced as Dexter pulled the silver Jaguar XF through the iron gates of the Rawlings estate. They were both dressed for the occasion. It seemed odd to be so formal and wearing a long gown, heels, and makeup with her hair styled added to her unease. She did find comfort in how handsome Dexter was in his tuxedo. This wasn't a large gathering. Just as she'd requested, there would only be the four of them, but nonetheless, it was the Rawlings estate.

Dexter's stare served as her reminder.

His hand reached across the console and squeezed hers. "You've done well on the telephone calls. It's time to face them." Every call, every word, had been said in Dexter's presence. He gave her the strength to carry through. The first time that Nat heard her mother's voice was the hardest. Natalie's stomach pinched, knowing that in a few moments she'd see her.

The large white house appeared as the trees parted. It too was beautiful and stately, the house her father had built for his queen. It was where her childhood was spent, but it was no longer her home. That was in Vermont.

Dexter and Natalie walked hand in hand up the front stairs. When the front door opened, Nat expected to see the familiar face of one of the staff. She didn't.

"Natalie!" Claire called as she raced forward and wrapped her daughter in her arms. When her mother finally pulled back, her emerald-green eyes were full of tears. To Natalie, her mother never aged, as beautiful today as the pictures of her when her parents first married. There had always been a large painting of her mother in her wedding dress adorning the wall above the fireplace in the sitting room. "Thank God. I've missed you so much."

Claire held tightly to Nat's hand as she turned to the man beside her daughter. "Hello, you must be Dexter Smithers."

He bowed his head respectfully. "Yes, ma'am. It's nice to meet you, Mrs. Rawlings."

Claire's cheeks rose. "That's rather formal from the man who stole my daughter's heart. Please, my name is Claire."

During their telephone calls, Nat reiterated the stories from the emails, how during her adventure of self-discovery, she'd met Dexter. At first, he'd helped her, staying with her and keeping her safe. With time, their relationship grew. Dexter was now the man she loved, the one she was engaged to marry. In reality, her stories were true. It was just their adventures that varied.

As they all stepped inside, three sets of eyes turned to the dominating footsteps of Nat's father entering the foyer. Dropping her mother's hand and stepping away from Dexter's possessive touch upon her lower back, Natalie ran to him and wrapped her arms around his neck. Without hesitation, he embraced her.

"Daddy."

"My little Nat. You had us all very worried." Even at his age, his deep voice summoned respect while commanding any situation.

She reached for her father's large hand and led him back to where Dexter and her mom stood. With her heart thumping, she stepped closer to Dexter and said, "Daddy, I want to introduce you to my fiancé."

Her father's shoulders broadened and neck stiffened. Before Natalie could say anything, her mother's petite hand landed upon her father's sleeve. As Claire's diamond ring glittered and prisms of rainbows danced, her touch served as a gentle reminder that this was not the time for Anthony Rawlings to assert his dominance.

Her father let out a long breath and offered his hand. "Hello, son. It's high time we finally meet you." The address was a statement of Anthony's position and age, not a term of endearment. This battle wasn't over. Anthony Rawlings didn't surrender.

"Sir," Dexter said.

"My husband, Nat's father...Mr. Rawlings," Claire said, introducing the two men. "Tony, this is Dexter."

"Dexter Smithers," Dexter repeated.

Tony's dark eyes narrowed. "Relation to Jonas?"

Surely he knew the truth. Anthony Rawlings would have known after the first time he saw Dexter's name. If he didn't know on sight, a search by his security would have been conducted and within moments the dots connected.

There was no reason for Dexter to deny it. "Yes, sir, his only son."

"We lost touch. I didn't know he had a son."

"Second wife. Only child, a little later in life. My father's no longer with us."

"I'm sorry to hear that," Tony said.

Natalie watched and listened as her father and Dexter spoke. She'd never heard about Dexter's family. She'd spoken about hers, but he'd never offered. Yet in merely seconds, her dad had shed more light than Dexter had offered in over five months.

"Dexter, can we offer you a drink before dinner?" Claire asked.

"Thank you, I'm not much of a drinker."

Tony nodded toward an archway. "Cognac. It's a man's drink."

"We also have water or soft drinks if you'd prefer," Claire offered.

As they all started walking toward the sitting room, Claire reached for Natalie's hand. "If you gentlemen will excuse us for a moment, I have a few things upstairs for Nat." She smiled. "Your Christmas gift."

Natalie looked to Dexter. She wasn't supposed to leave his side or speak out of his sight. He'd made the rules crystal clear. Failure to abide by them would result in a stay in the basement room. It was truly her biggest nightmare. She'd willingly take the sting of his belt or a crop. It usually resulted with him inside her and the relief that only he can bring her. The room and all it represented was something else. It meant being alone or—as she'd learned—worse, not being alone.

The panic may have shown in her gaze until he grinned and kissed her cheek. "Hurry back."

"I hate to leave you."

Dexter shook his head. "I'll be fine, bug."

The tendons in her father's neck stretched at the sound of Dexter's demeaning nickname.

"Be nice, Daddy," Nat said.

"Of course..." His deep voice echoed through the foyer. "Dexter, join me in the sitting room while they catch up. We have things to discuss."

As she walked up the stairs with her mother, Natalie looked back down toward the room that held her fiancé and her father. "Mom, do you think they'll be all right?"

Claire smiled. "For a short time." She then went on, chatting about Natalie, how beautiful she looked, how handsome Dexter was... She asked about the sights Natalie had visited and then when they reached her parents' room, Claire led Nat inside and shut the door.

As the latch closed, her mother's emerald eyes no longer shone. There was darkness in their depths that stung Natalie with a bite worse than the slap of a crop. Somehow, in this brief span of time, her mother knew. She knew Nat's secrets... knew what happened behind closed doors.

"Is he good to you?" Claire asked.

Natalie shifted, finding it difficult to keep her mother's gaze. "He can be, Mom. He really can."

Claire's eyes closed as her face momentarily fell forward. When she looked back up, Natalie's eyes were wet. Claire wrapped her daughter in her arms. "Tell me if you love him."

"I do. I can't explain it. Please don't ask me to."

"I don't need to ask. I understand."

Natalie's head shook. "I don't think you do. It's not like you and Dad."

Taking a step back, Claire sighed. "Oh, my baby. Someday when you have children, you'll understand the struggle. Parents are complicated. We play such a vital role in our children's lives. Sometimes we keep secrets hidden to protect, but it seems that it doesn't always protect; it leaves the door open, an invitation to those who lie in wait."

"I'm not sure what you're talking about."

"Does he value your feelings and opinions?"

It was a strange question, yet Nat answered. "He wants them. He's always asking me to tell him how I feel and what I'm thinking."

Claire smiled. "That took your father longer."

"Mom?"

"I love you, Natalie Rawlings. I always will."

"I know, Mom. I love you, too."

"Your father does too. We also love one another."

Natalie slapped her hands against her side as she let out an exasperated breath. "I know. I always thought I wanted what you have, but then with Dexter..."

Claire reached for her daughter's hand and led her to a small sofa where they sat. "This may not make a lot of sense right now, but please let me try to explain."

Nat nodded.

"When I found a man I loved more than life itself and whose love for me was overwhelming, I was alone. I didn't have my mother to talk to or to give me her support. I'm not unhappy with the final result, but let me just say that the journey would've been easier if I wouldn't have made it alone. I know you aren't ready to hear or say more. I can see it in your eyes.

They're mine. They always have been, different from Nate's and so much different from Nichol's. Natalie, you are me."

"I'm not..." A tear trickled from her freshly painted eyes as her words faded away.

"You are. The question I asked—if he's good to you—was the same question your Uncle John asked me a long time ago. You answered it exactly as I did."

"Mom?"

"No matter what I need to do," Claire said, "I want you *and Dexter* to know that I won't judge you. I won't lose my baby or her babies. Your father will be more difficult—he is—but leave him to me. Please promise me that no matter what the future holds, no matter your last name, you'll always be a Rawlings."

"I don't know about my name. Dexter and I haven't discussed..."

Claire smiled. "I don't mean your legal name. I've suspected from your emails, but seeing you, I know."

"Know what?"

"I know that you have a man in your life. One who consumes your thoughts, who takes up most of the room in your heart, but, baby, there's always room for more. I know, because there was a time I believed your father was my every-thing. It's not that he wasn't or isn't. It's that each time I learned that I was going to have a child, my heart grew. The same will happen for you. I'm just asking that you also keep a spot for us —for your family and especially for me. No matter what, I'll be there."

Natalie leaned into her mother's embrace. "I love you, Mom."

After their hug, Claire rose and walked to a bookshelf, reaching for a small box with a ribbon. She came back and handed it to Natalie. "Merry belated Christmas."

Nat's eyes watered as she opened the hinged box to the delicate necklace. "It's like yours and Nichol's necklaces." A small pearl sat nestled in a white-gold X.

"It is. I'm not sure why we never had one made for you before. But when you weren't at Christmas, I realized how much the necklace means to me and to your sister. Your father and I gave your great-grandmother's necklace to Nichol when she was young. It was your dad who surprised me by having one remade for me. It's more special that I can even articulate."

Claire smiled as she touched Nat's hand. "Yours and mine are identical; they're replicas. That doesn't make them less than Nichol's. It makes ours the same, like us. I can see it in your eyes and hear it in your voice. Natalie, you're no longer our baby."

"I'm not."

"You're a beautiful woman and always know that we're proud of you." She lifted Nat's left hand and looked at the ring. "That's beautiful. He loves you, too."

"He does." Nat's cheeks filled with pink as her heart swelled. "Thank you, Mom. I was afraid that after Harvard—"

Claire squeezed her hand. "Sometimes our lives take a detour. Though at first it may seem wrong, it can provide an opportunity to live a life different than we ever imagined. Are you happy with where yours took you?"

"Yes."

"Then that's all that matters. I have another gift for you, but right now, let's go back downstairs. I think it might be beneficial to keep your father and Dexter supervised."

CHAPTER 26

*Acceptance of what has happened is the
first step to overcoming the consequences...* ~ William James

A few weeks later, back in Vermont, Dexter entered their master bedroom suite.

Wearing only one of his shirts, Natalie rose and met her fiancé at the door.

Dexter kissed her hair. "What have you been doing this evening?"

She looked at him through veiled eyes. "Reading."

Reading didn't require a submissive gaze. Something wasn't

as it appeared. His eyes went to the sofa where she'd been seated. His neck tensed, the muscles becoming rigid as his gaze landed upon the book she'd been reading. "Where did you get that?"

"My mother."

"Your mother?"

Natalie went to the sofa and lifted the old book. The pages were yellow and the spine was marred with the scars of multiple readings. On the cover was the title: *My Life as It Didn't Appear.*

"Your mother gave you that?"

Natalie nodded.

"Why?"

She shrugged. "I guess she decided I wasn't a baby who needed to be protected anymore. She thought it was time I knew the truth."

The book, *My Life as It Didn't Appear,* dictated by Claire Nichols Rawlings and penned by Meredith Banks, detailed Claire Nichols's meeting and first marriage to Anthony Rawlings. Upon its publication, it had been an instant bestseller. Through years of legal wrangling, which concluded over fifteen years ago, the Rawlings attorneys successfully had it removed from sale and circulation. The world forgot, ceasing to obsess over old news. There were more important stories. And through it all, somehow, Nat's parents had managed to keep its existence, as well as its contents, hidden from their baby girl.

"And how does it make you feel about your father?" Dexter asked.

"You know what it's about?"

"Bug."

Her entire body stiffened. He'd asked her a question. Instead

213

of answering, she'd replied with her own question. Natalie quickly re-spoke, "No different."

"How can you say that?"

"How can I not?" Natalie replied. "And before you reprimand me, that *is* an answer. I don't feel differently. Why would I?"

Dexter led her to the sofa and they sat. "What do you mean?"

"How could I think less of him when I love you?"

It took Dexter a minute, but then he let go of her hand and went to the bookcase. Behind a false panel—one that she didn't know existed—Dexter brought out a copy of the same book.

Natalie shook her head as she reached for it. "How?"

"I found it among my father's things after he died." Dexter opened the cover and pulled out a yellowed piece of paper. "And this."

Natalie silently read. It wasn't legal, no binding contract. It was simply an agreement between college friends. They'd begun a company: CSR-Company Smithers Rawlings. Together they vowed to make it great, uniting their families and lives forever.

"What happened?" Nat asked.

"After a few years your father bought mine out. It was very amicable. Mr. Rawlings paid my father a generous sum. They both went on to do very well. You know about your father. Mine took the money and started investing in real estate. It wasn't the buyout. It was the part about keeping the two families united that got me thinking. My mother was also gone, so I didn't have a family. I wanted one. Then I read the book and looked into the Rawlings family. That was when I knew..."

Natalie laid the book on the sofa and fell to her knees. Her bare core clenched as she scooted between his spread legs.

Looking up, she spoke. "It was when you knew I belonged to you...that we were meant to be a family?"

"Yes, bug. That we belonged together. I knew what I wanted, what I needed. And after watching you for a while, I knew in my heart that you were born to be my queen."

"But my dad..." It wasn't easy for her to read the things her father had done to her mother. It was even more difficult to say them. "...she awoke to luxury?"

"Is that a question?"

"I think it is."

"I didn't use your mother's story as a guide. It simply gave me an idea of how you'd respond. Think about it. Your mother came from a simple life. Your father gave her what she'd never experienced."

Natalie nodded. "A detour. I came from wealth—from everything."

"And did you appreciate it?"

"No, not really. It just was. I didn't question it. I appreciate it more now."

Dexter kissed her hair. "I love you, Nat. Do you think that one day you'd want to write down our story for our daughter to read?"

Her cheeks warmed. "No, I'd rather keep it in my heart. But if one day I think she needs to hear it, I'll share."

"You will?"

"I will. It helps to know that there isn't anything wrong with me. I'm not the only one to experience these feelings."

"What feelings?"

"Love so overpowering it consumes me. An irrational yet intoxicating need to both please you and make you happy that supersedes all else, even my own safety."

"No. Your safety was never and will never be in question. I

told you that safety is a matter of trust. Do you trust me?"

"I do." After all of the things he'd done and all that she willingly accepted, how could she not?

"Danger," Dexter went on, "is something else. However, eliciting your tears doesn't put you in danger. It's never to *harm* you. It's to *hurt* you. There's a difference. What we do is controlled pain, learning how much you can handle, how much you're willing to sacrifice for me. It's seeing my marks on your skin and hearing your cries. That doesn't make me want to harm you, but to worship you."

Nat nodded. "I understand. After a few weeks in that room, I found myself anxious for your arrival while at the same time scared. I feared I was going crazy. I mean, I shouldn't have wanted what I knew you'd do." She looked at the book. "Now I know that I'm not crazy. Like my mom has said: *it is what it is. Don't fight what you can't change.* Now it makes more sense.

"It's what we enjoy behind closed doors. And that's okay." She smiled. "You asked what I'd sacrifice. For you, my king, anything." She knew in her heart there were no limits. "I'd move naked into the room in our basement if you desired."

Dexter's eyes shone as he reached for the buttons lining the front of her shirt-dress. "I think I like having you here in our room, naked and on your knees."

Relief washed through her as she leaned back on her bent toes, shifting to his desired position. "I love you."

After he'd opened her shirt-dress, he looked down to her spread legs. "Are you wet, my queen?"

"Yes."

"What will you do to earn the right to come?"

Her heart hammered within her chest as her thighs glistened. "Like everything else, that decision is yours. I willingly give you control. As always, my answer is anything."

CHAPTER 27

Isn't life a series of images that change
as they repeat themselves? ~ Andy Warhol

Taylor walked a step behind her husband as they moved about the century-old villa high in the mountains of Austria. It had taken them too long to find it—too much time. Their inability to find all the pieces had worked to Dexter Smithers's advantage.

The problem they encountered was that the name on the long-ago deed wasn't Smithers. Dexter's wealth originating from his father wasn't only from the investments his father made with the money Anthony Rawlings paid him for his half of CSR Corporation. Jonas Smithers, Dexter's father, had once been married to a Becker. The Beckers were an established wealthy family living in Austria, in this villa. Due to a string of unfortunate events, his first wife lived here with her extended family when she was young.

When Solana Smithers died, she and Jonas had no children. The rest of her family was gone.

Her family tree was warped and convoluted and had finally died out. No wonder it took Phil and Taylor time to untwist the branches.

Generations before Jonas's wife was born, there were two Becker brothers who had a falling out, according to stories Phil and Taylor had uncovered. One brother stayed in Austria and claimed the family name and wealth. The other moved to the States and began his entrepreneurial endeavors dealing in the sale of cars. At the time, there was a bright future in the world of auto sales in America. Never able to have children, Hans Becker was elated to marry a woman with one son. His wife's son and he worked side by side. Though his stepson never took the Becker name, he carried on the business of the only man to ever be his father.

By all accounts, Richard London, Hans Becker's stepson, was a proud and honest man. It wasn't until a series of misfortunes in the mid-1980s that his dreams of prosperity were torn to shreds. His wife's brother moved into their home. As an addict, her brother eventually ended up in prison. Drugs fuel a need that the body can't do without, even enticing the addict to commit crimes for the next hit. The family fell into further disgrace when Richard's oldest daughter became pregnant.

Very little is known about that time in Richard London's life. Some say his oldest daughter died. Others say she was shunned. Even her first name has been stricken from the family records. Only the initial M remains. The few leads have come up with multiple possibilities of this woman's identity.

Taylor and Phil planned to do more digging. Currently, their focus had been on Natalie and Jonas Dexter Smithers.

It was nearly five years after Richard's daughter's disappearance—or death, depending on the source—when Richard's auto business in upstate New York failed. Even that was suspicious. The seemingly thriving business fell into bankruptcy. Richard's life was in a tailspin. His wife left him without warning. His health was suffering. All Richard had left was his youngest daughter. Out of desperation for her welfare, he contacted the family he'd only heard about in Europe.

Richard wanted more for his only remaining child than he could provide.

Thankfully, his distant relatives welcomed the girl. To them it was a blessing. They welcomed her into their home and lives as the daughter they never had. After Richard's death, they adopted her, making her a Becker by law.

Solana Becker and Jonas married many years later. Some say that she was the reason CSR Corporation was divided. Though Anthony and Jonas remained cordial, apparently, Solana Smithers and Anthony Rawlings didn't get along.

Six years after Jonas and Anthony mutually agreed to part ways, Solana was taken by an aggressive form of brain cancer. Though Jonas wasn't interested in the villa and wealth Solana had inherited, it became his. Jonas also wasn't interested in remarrying, not until he met Serena Bower.

Younger than Jonas, Serena gave him what he'd never imagined he'd have, a son—Jonas Dexter Smithers.

As the leaves of the Smithers family tree fluttered to the ground around Taylor and Phil's feet, a sickening sense of déjà vu came to Phil. The sidebar of the London connection made his skin crawl. He hadn't taken the story of Dexter's family history to Rawlings yet. First, Phil needed to do more research. The name London was rather common and as of yet, the M standing for the name Marie had not been confirmed or discounted.

Nevertheless, as they untangled the history of Dexter's family, Phil and Taylor discovered the villa in the mountains of Austria.

A few euros to the right staff member and now they were walking the halls of the home where they were certain Natalie had been living. The Becker and later Smithers wealth was evident. The villa was luxurious, lovely, and secluded. As Frau Schmitt recalled stories of a quiet, beautiful young girl, Phil's fears waned.

It wasn't until they went to the lower level that Phil's gut told him there were secrets to learn. He was good at watching people, reading their nonverbal cues. As they entered the large library and media room in the lower level, Frau Schmitt's eyes had grown wide.

He scanned the layout. The room was more modern than most of the house. The trim at the far end of the room, while ornate, was newer, of a different aged wood than the rest of the villa.

"Is there a problem?" he asked in broken German.

She shook her head. "Nein."

Step by step, he and Taylor inspected the room. With each passing minute, Frau Schmitt seemed to grow more and more agitated, repeating her request for them to go.

The hinges on the panel within the far wall were barely visible. Yet they were there. And neatly hidden along the trim was a small keyhole.

"Where's the key?" Phil asked Frau Schmitt.

"I don't know. We aren't even supposed to be down here. I'm not." Her newfound ability to speak English was difficult to decipher. She'd initially appeared to understand only German. "I didn't know there was a door," she added.

"Why aren't you supposed to be here?" Taylor asked.

"Herr Smithers doesn't allow it. This is his space."

Despite Frau Schmitt's protests, Taylor searched the bookcases and cabinets as Phil continued to inspect the door. He wasn't sure, but with such a small keyhole, he wondered if the locking mechanism wasn't more involved.

And if it was, why?

Only slightly out of alignment with the other books on the shelf, Taylor removed what appeared to be a ragged copy of an old classic. The book was lighter than it should have been, merely a case disguised as a book. Within it, she found a key ring with what appeared to be a car fob attached.

When she handed it to Phil, he asked, "Why would Herr Smithers keep his car keys down here and hidden?"

Frau Schmitt shook her head. "I don't know. I've never seen those before."

Slowly, Phil stepped to the panel and inserted the key. It fit.

A series of clicks told him that he'd been right. The one key opened more than one deadbolt hidden within the thick door, working together to keep the panel locked in place. Pulling on the key, the wood barrier opened toward him, into the room and away from a dark hallway. Reaching inside he noticed the decrease in temperature as he found a light switch.

Though Frau Schmitt refused to go any farther, Taylor was now beside her husband as they stepped into the cool tunnel, a stark contrast to the rest of the house. A musty aroma hung in the air. Everything blended—very plain, stark gray, both sides of the hall having been constructed of cement blocks with a concrete floor.

Within the hallway were two doors. Phil opened the first. Switching on the light he found a narrow utility closet. There was a small round folding table and two chairs. There was a cabinet, also locked. The key in his hand didn't open the doors.

He and Taylor moved to the other door. It was a door, but it wasn't. It was more like a piece of heavy wood, painted white that didn't have a handle.

Phil pushed against the new barrier. Once, twice, his body's weight did nothing to budge it.

"Phil, the fob," Taylor said.

Phil's eyes closed. He didn't want to open this door. It was the same way he felt reading Meredith's book *My Life as It Didn't Appear*. Once he opened the cover, he couldn't stop reading and learning the secrets behind Claire and Mr. Rawlings's relationship. That book forever altered his opinions. If this door opened, he'd always know the secrets that might be better left buried.

"Phil?" Taylor laid her hand on his arm. "I'll do it."

This was his job. No. This was his family. He shook his head as he pushed the button.

A beep echoed through the hallway.

The door creaked opened on its own.

"Oh my God," Taylor gasped as Phil pushed it farther. "You don't think...?"

He couldn't pull his eyes away from the only piece of furniture within the room. It was a bed, more the size of a cot, with a thin mattress. The room was tall, extending up to a narrow window. Another button on the fob turned on lights hidden near the ceiling.

The illumination did little to enhance the room. Everything was white, except the concrete gray floor.

"There's a bathroom over here," Taylor said. She turned back to her husband. "Why do you think this place is here? You don't think...Natalie?"

Phil shook his head. "I don't want to."

"She looked healthy and content at the airport. That's why I didn't intervene."

Phil agreed. "I saw her when they came to the estate. The surveillance we have set up outside Smithers's place in Vermont shows her coming and going."

Taylor touched his arm again. "She always looks happy. This can't be what we're thinking."

"Please, come out," Frau Schmitt called from the finished area outside this...prison cell. "Herr Smithers will not be pleased."

Phil removed his phone and began snapping pictures.

"Are we going to tell Mr. Rawlings and Claire?"

"I can't imagine what this would do to them," Phil answered. "What it would do to her."

"Then let's be sure before we say anything."

Phil nodded.

The room was bare. Everything had been cleaned or removed. There were no towels in the bathroom or sheets on the cot.

Taylor reached down to the drain of the bathtub. There wasn't much and it was dry, having been there for a while. She held out her hand.

Strands of long brown hair.

"It might not be hers," Taylor offered.

Phil's lips came together as he shook his head. "Keep it. We'll have a DNA test run."

Taylor pulled a small evidence bag from her tote.

"Why Natalie?" Taylor asked Phil later in their hotel suite, though they still didn't know for certain.

His stomach was in knots. Another Rawlings woman he'd failed. "I can't even venture to surmise. But as we learn more about Dexter Smithers's family, it seems like ripples on a pond, the circle keeps going on and on. We just need to learn who threw the first stone."

"We'll learn. We won't give up."

CHAPTER 28

You can close your eyes to reality but not to memories~ Stanislaw
Jerzy Lec

Claire shook her head in disbelief as Tony's fingers blanched, his grip tightening on the arms of the chair. The story Phil was telling them was too contrived to be real and yet too unbelievable to be fiction.

"I never remember her mentioning a sister. But then again, she never spoke about her family, not to me. Did Dexter even know Marie? She died almost ten years ago," Tony said.

It wasn't that they made a point of following Marie

London's prison sentence; however, each time she came up for parole, the Rawlingses were there. The first time it happened, Tony insisted on going alone. He said he didn't want Claire to have to face her. Claire disagreed. Marie played a significant role in her life as well as Tony's. She stated her case. In the end, she went. At each subsequent hearing, they went together. Their legal teams constructed letters appealing for the denial of her parole. Even when she became ill, the Rawlingses petitioned for her to remain in prison, where she belonged.

There may have been other factors at work to keep Marie incarcerated. Tony had a knack for getting his way. Claire didn't want to know. She simply wanted justice. The day they received the message that she had passed away within a federal penitentiary hospital was the day Claire finally let go of the fear that someday Marie would find a way to harm her family.

Had she done it? Had Marie somehow had influence over Dexter? Were his motives something other than they appeared?

"He would have been so young," Claire said.

"We can't make a connection," Phil said. "That's why this has been so elusive. We've scoured the visitor records at the penitentiary. He never visited. Not under his own name. She had very few visitors over the years.

"The most obvious connection between Jonas Dexter Smithers and the Rawlings family, besides now Natalie, is with his father and you."

Tony reached for a pencil resting upon his desk and snapped it in two. "Me. I brought that man into our daughter's life. The man who calls her bug. What the hell kind of name is that?"

It was a rhetorical question, one Tony had voiced more than once since Dexter and Natalie's visit.

"Mrs. Rawlings," Taylor said. "May we talk for a minute?"

Claire nodded.

"No, outside the office."

Claire looked about the room, her green eyes scanning Taylor, Phil, and finally Tony. "No. We can talk here."

"Claire," Phil said, "I'd like to show something to Mr. Rawlings."

Her pulse quickened and stomach twisted. "If this has to do with Nat, I want to see it."

"Maybe..." Tony began.

She could barely hear her husband over the rush of blood in her ears. The mother's intuition she'd felt the day they received the first text message, the day Natalie had not made it to Nice, was back. "I'm going to say this one time: if you have anything to say about my daughter, you'll say it in front of me."

Taylor walked closer to Claire. "It's not going to be easy to see. Maybe if Mr. Rawlings saw it first, he could help you."

"I'm not sure how fragile you think I am, but I can tell you that I've survived more than what you can show me."

"Yes, Claire, you have," Phil said, "but this is Nat."

"And she's alive and well in Vermont. I wish she were here, but I know she's safe. If you were going to show me something and I didn't know that she was safe, then I could understand the concern. She's safe."

Tony's head shook as he muttered, "In Vermont, but safe?"

Phil nodded. "That's what we need to discuss."

"Listen, I may not agree with everything that happens, but I will support my daughter no matter what. I've said it before: I will not lose her."

After Phil and Taylor exchanged glances, Phil opened his iPad and pulled up pictures. Tony and Claire stood and moved closer. No one spoke as the first picture came into view. It was of a large, lovely villa, almost castle-like, surrounded by pine trees.

"Is this where she was?" Tony asked, his jaw clenched.

"Yes, we confirmed it with a staff member," Taylor answered. "She identified Natalie in pictures."

"It's big." It was the only thing Claire could think to say. It seemed as though she'd been in a lovely place. Claire wanted to believe that. However, Tony's original home had been beautiful too. Though it had been leveled decades ago, there were still pictures. For some reason, the picture from the article about them in Vanity Fair came to her mind.

"It is large," Phil said. "One of the things that caught our attention was that the staff member informed us that Natalie had been with Herr Smithers for just over a month."

Claire stood taller as her lips came together.

"A month?" Tony asked. "Where was she before that? You said it was Diane, not Nat traveling. Where was Nat?"

Phil swiped the screen to the next picture.

Claire gasped, her knees going weak as a wave of nausea washed through her.

Tony reached for her arm, steadying her, yet unable to look away from the screen. He pulled his wife closer. "He's going to die."

Claire shook her head. "No, this isn't what we're thinking."

"The room had been cleaned, but we found a hair in the drain of the tub."

"A long brown hair," Taylor emphasized, confirming what Phil had just said. "We had it tested. It was Natalie's."

As Tony swore under his breath, Claire reached for the iPad and walked back to the sofa. Her nausea wouldn't allow her to stand any longer. Yet she couldn't look away, not now that she'd seen.

She swiped the screen, over and over, taking in the small

room from different angles. There were pictures of the stark bathroom with an old clawfoot bathtub. "In this drain?"

"Yes," Taylor confirmed. "The room is now empty, as you can see. There are no sheets, blankets, or towels...or clothes. There were also no clothes in the master bedroom. There really is no way to know exactly what happened."

"She was taken. We were right," Claire said, looking to Tony, her voice cracking. "But why like this? Why?"

"We're going to Vermont and bringing her home."

"I want to see her again, to know she's safe. I think I already knew how their relationship was, but I never...I can't imagine..." Her green eyes overflowed with tears. "...how could I even fathom?"

"How much are you willing to spend to change the playing field?" Phil asked.

"As much as it takes," Tony replied.

Claire blinked away the tears. "What are you talking about?"

"Dexter Smithers thinks he can hide behind his fortune. If it's gone, he can't hide."

Claire thought back, memories she hadn't entertained in decades coming to the surface. "He can't know it's you. If he does, she'll be the one to pay."

Tony nodded. "I hate that you're thinking that way, but you're right. Don't worry. He won't know what hit him."

"And Nat? What if she truly loves him?"

"Then he needs to earn it, not take it."

Claire took a deep breath and slowly let it out. "I know that, too." She looked into her husband's dark stare. "It could still happen. After a terrible beginning, it could happen. She could forgive him. They could be happy."

"Then he better be ready to pay the price and earn her

forgiveness. He needs to want it too, enough to work for it. To admit what he's done and let Nat be the one who decides."

"I guess time will tell."

Tony swallowed, his eyes silently repeating the apology Claire refused to allow his lips to utter. He'd said it many times, but now they were beyond that. Their past was over. They'd moved on. Life was too short to harbor resentment over the past.

Yet at times like this, as Claire settled against the couch, the memories were more vivid than they'd been the day before. The colors were still real. Closing her eyes, she saw the white woodwork of her suite and the black of his eyes.

As Tony and Phil began to discuss options, Claire's cell phone rang. Their daughter's name appeared on the screen. "It's Nat." She wiped her cheeks. "I have to talk to her. I never know when she'll call again."

The other three all nodded.

"Invite her home," Tony suggested.

"Okay..." Claire worked to steady her tone.

CHAPTER 29

The trust of the innocent
is the liar's most useful tool. ~ Stephen King

"Nat, it's so good to hear your voice."

"Mom," Nat said, smiling at her fiancé as she spoke through the speaker of the phone. "I'm just calling about the wedding. Will next month work for you and Dad?"

"It's a lot to plan. Maybe you could come home and help?"

Dexter's hand splayed over her bare thigh. She used to get completely dressed before calling her mother. It seemed odd to be talking to them wearing only one of Dexter's shirts. But over time, it no longer bothered her. This is how she often was. When she spoke on the phone, it didn't make sense to don an outfit first.

Dexter shook his head and grinned, encouraging her to say what they'd already discussed, to stay the course he'd determined.

"Mom, we've decided we don't want to wait any longer, and we want it small. Just family and very close friends. I'd love to have Phil and Taylor, and of course the Simmonses, and Uncle John and Aunt Emily. But not all of Dad's associates."

"I'm sure we can plan it," Claire said.

"The thing is, we want to get married at our house."

"Oh." The disappointment was evident in her mother's sigh.

"Will you and Daddy come out to Vermont?"

"Yes," Claire answered quickly.

Nat looked at Dexter. His expression was one of satisfaction, one she adored. "Good. If you can visit soon, we can make the final plans together."

"Of course, Nat. Tell Dexter we said hello. Remember, I love you, and we're here." She seemed to pause. "The most important thing is that you're happy."

"I am, Mom."

Nat's insides pinched as Dexter signaled for her to end the call. "I need to go. I'll talk to you later." Her mind went to their upcoming *Dexter-time* as anticipation flooded her body.

"When would you like us to come?"

Nat smiled, certain she heard her father's voice in the background saying they'd get on a plane today. "Next week."

"What day do you want us next week?"

Nat looked to her fiancé. "Day, next week?" Dexter mouthed the word as Nat spoke it, "Wednesday. Wednesday would be great. Dexter can take a few days away from the office."

"We'll be there."

"Bye, Mom."

"Are you sure you couldn't come home sooner? Your dad can send a plane."

Nat shook her head. "Mom, next week is good. I'll talk to you again."

"Okay. Goodbye, dear."

After disconnecting the call, she handed Dexter the phone.

His finger traced the edge of her chin. "Bug, you knew it was Wednesday."

"I forgot."

"That's not acceptable."

"I was too busy thinking about you."

He shook his head as his finger trailed down the gap left by the open buttons on his shirt. When Dexter reached her breasts, he traced each one, over and over, until her nipples became hard nubs. He looked up with a smile on his face. "What am I going to do with you?"

"Whatever you want, my king."

"Marry you and announce to the world that you're mine."

"I am yours," Natalie Rawlings confirmed. "Forever."

"Forever."

Thank you for reading Natalie and Dexter's story, the story of how they found one another. Ripples was meant to be a stand-alone novel, and as their story, it is. Perhaps in time, we'll learn more about them, their future, and the rest of the Rawlings family if Nichol's or Nate's story ever presents itself to me. Please let me know if you'd be interested in more.

Thank you!

FOR MORE

If you haven't read the beginning of this story...if this was your first introduction to Tony and Claire Rawlings or maybe you began their story but didn't complete it, it's not too late.

The Consequences series is five full-length books: Consequences, Truth, Convicted, Revealed, and Beyond the Consequences. For more insight into Tony Rawlings, after the series has been read, there are two companions: Behind His Eyes Consequences and Behind His Eyes Truth. Book one, Consequences, is free on all channels.

Thank you for reading Natalie and Dexter's story, Ripples, a story where physical chains are more freeing than figurative ones, and in finding a new life, the princess becomes the queen.

I hope you enjoyed the consequences...

LINK to Consequences series on all platforms:

https://www.aleatharomig.com/consequences-series

The individual links can be found under Books by New York Times bestselling author Aleatha Romig in the table of contents.

WHAT TO DO NOW

LEND IT: Did you enjoy RIPPLES? Do you have a friend who'd enjoy RIPPLES? The eBook of RIPPLES may be lent one time. Sharing is caring!

RECOMMEND IT: Do you have multiple friends who'd enjoy RIPPLES? Tell them about it! Call, text, post, tweet...your recommendation is the nicest gift you can give to an author!

REVIEW IT: Tell the world. Please go to the retailer where you purchased this book, as well as Goodreads, and write a review. Please share your thoughts about RIPPLES on:

*Amazon, *RIPPLES*, Customer Reviews

*Barnes & Noble, *RIPPLES*, Customer Reviews

*iBooks, *RIPPLES*, Customer Reviews

*Goodreads.com/Aleatha Romig

BOOKS BY NEW YORK TIMES BESTSELLING AUTHOR ALEATHA ROMIG

ALEATHA'S LIGHTER ONES:

PLUS ONE

Stand-alone fun, sexy romance

Released May 2017

ONE NIGHT

Stand-alone, sexy contemporary romance

Coming September 2017

THE INFIDELITY SERIES:

BETRAYAL

Book #1

(October 2015)

CUNNING

Book #2

(January 2016)

DECEPTION

Book #3

(May 2016)

ENTRAPMENT

Book #4

(September 2016)

FIDELITY

Book #5

(January 2017)

RESPECT

A stand-alone Infidelity novel

(Coming January 2018)

THE CONSEQUENCES SERIES:

CONSEQUENCES

(Book #1)

Released August 2011

TRUTH

(Book #2)

Released October 2012

CONVICTED

(Book #3)

Released October 2013

REVEALED

(Book #4)

Previously titled: Behind His Eyes Convicted: The Missing Years

Re-released June 2014

BEYOND THE CONSEQUENCES

(Book #5)

Released January 2015Released January 2015

CONSEQUENCES COMPANION READS:

BEHIND HIS EYES-CONSEQUENCES

Released January 2014

BEHIND HIS EYES-TRUTH

Released March 2014

THE LIGHT SERIES:

Published through Thomas and Mercer Amazon exclusive

INTO THE LIGHT

Released 2016

AWAY FROM THE DARK

Released 2016

TALES FROM THE DARK SIDE SERIES:

INSIDIOUS

(All books in this series are stand-alone erotic thrillers)

Released October 2014

DUPLICITY

(Completely unrelated to book #1)

Release TBA

ABOUT THE AUTHOR

ALEATHA ROMIG

Aleatha Romig is a New York Times, Wall Street Journal, and USA Today bestselling author who lives in Indiana, USA. She grew up in Mishawaka, graduated from Indiana University, and is currently living south of Indianapolis. Aleatha has raised three children with her high school sweetheart and husband of over thirty years. Before she became a full-time author, she worked days as a dental hygienist and spent her nights writing. Now, when she's not imagining mind-blowing twists and turns, she likes to spend her time a with her family and friends. Her other pastimes include reading and creating heroes/anti-heroes who haunt your dreams!

Aleatha released her first novel, CONSEQUENCES, in August of 2011. CONSEQUENCES became a bestselling series with five novels and two companions released from 2011 through 2015. The compelling and epic story of Anthony and Claire Rawlings has graced more than half a million e-readers. Aleatha released the first of her series TALES FROM THE DARK SIDE, INSIDIOUS, in the fall of 2014. These stand alone thrillers continue Aleatha's twisted style with an increase in heat.

In the fall of 2015, Aleatha moved head first into the world of dark romantic suspense with the release of BETRAYAL, the first of her five novel INFIDELITY series that has taken the reading world by storm. She also began her traditional publishing career with Thomas and Mercer. Her books INTO THE LIGHT and AWAY FROM THE DARK were published through this mystery/thriller publisher in 2016.

2017 brings Aleatha's first "Leatha, the lighter side of Aleatha" with PLUS ONE, a fun, sexy romantic comedy.

Aleatha is a "Published Author's Network" member of the Romance Writers of America and PEN America. She is represented by Kevan Lyon of Marsal Lyon Literary Agency.

Stay connected with Aleatha

Do you love Aleatha's writing? Do you want to keep up to date about what's coming next?

Do you like EXCLUSIVE content (never-released scenes, never-released excerpts, and more)? Would you like the monthly chance to win prizes (signed books and gift cards)? Then sign up today for Aleatha's monthly newsletter and stay informed on all things Aleatha Romig.

NEWSLETTER: Recipients of Aleatha's Newsletter receive exclusive material and offers.

Aleatha's Newsletter Sign-up

You can also find Aleatha@

Goodreads:
http://www.goodreads.com/author/show/5131072.Aleatha_R omig

Instagram: http://instagram.com/aleatharomig
You may also listen to Aleatha Romig books on Audible:
Aleatha's Audibles

www.aleatharomig.com
aleatharomig@gmail.com

CPSIA information can be obtained
at www.ICGtesting.com
Printed in the USA
LVHW081616290719
625731LV00014B/1135/P